The Rose Petal
Rags and Riches

by C. Casarico

191 Bank Street
Burlington, Vermont 05401

Onion River Press
191 Bank Street
Burlington, VT 05401

ISBN: 978-0-9976458-6-6
Library of Congress Control Number: 2018963948

Printed in the United States of America

Cover Design © CEO Inked Creations
Images Used:
© Konstantin Yuganov / Adobe Stock
© Brian Jackson/ Adobe Stock

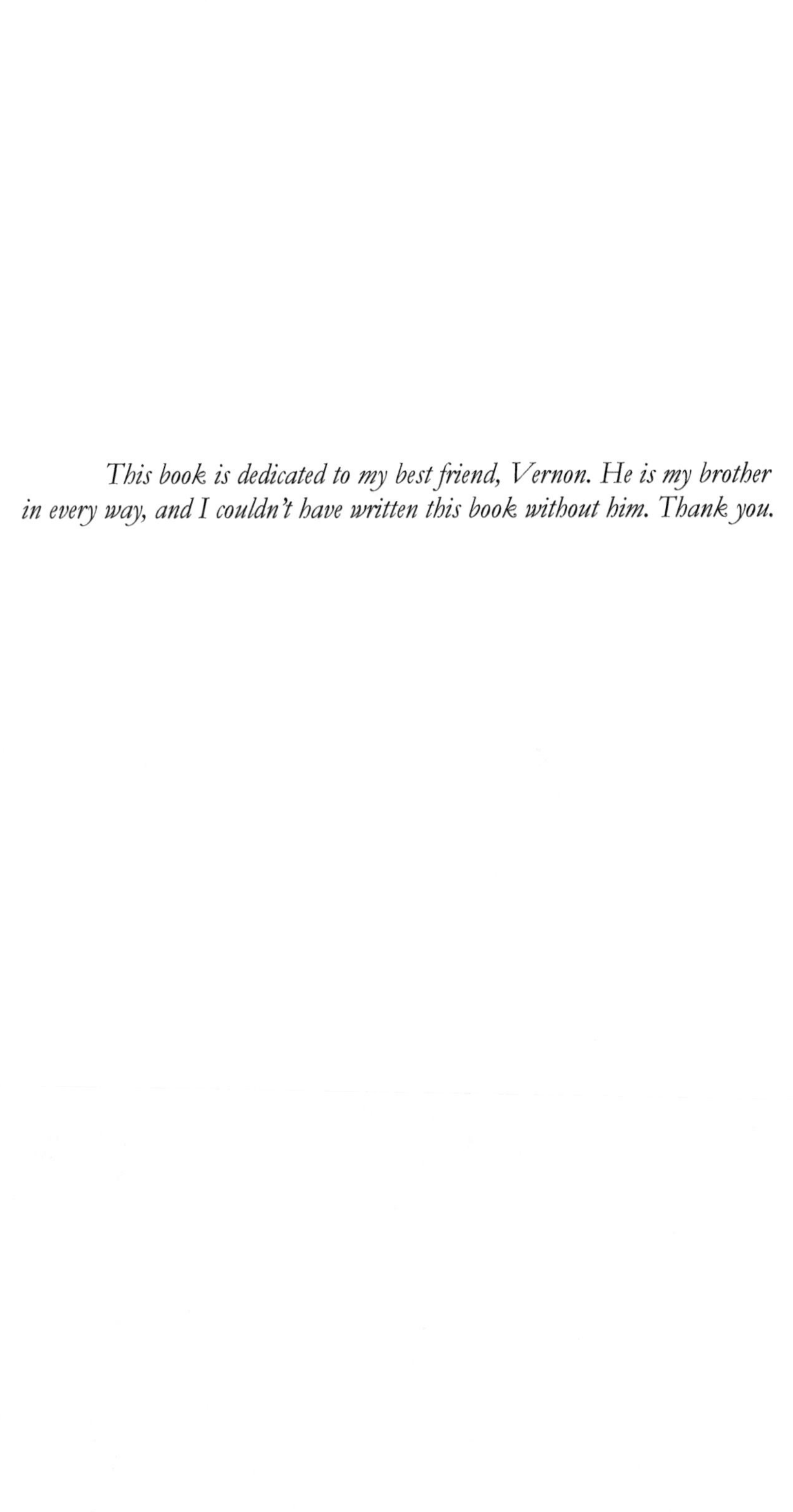

This book is dedicated to my best friend, Vernon. He is my brother in every way, and I couldn't have written this book without him. Thank you.

Part 1

Chapter 1: New Friends

I sighed as I jiggled the bag on my knee. It seemed to get heavier and heavier by the minute. The clock above the fireplace ticked away slowly.

Thinking of what was in my bag, I sighed again. The blank book my dad wanted me to use as a journal, seemed to be the heaviest thing in it. I didn't think I would ever know why he kept insisting I keep a journal. Unlike him, I wasn't a writer. I didn't spend hours at my desk scribbling in notebooks, or talk about characters who existed only in my mind. That was his world, which he wanted to force on me. I shook my head, annoyed. On some levels my father was crazy, but he did care about me.

Unable to stay still, I pulled the blank book out of my bag. There were about a hundred pages in it. It was a spiral notebook with a dark-green background. On the front cover was a gold star encircled by a shimmering gold circle.

"The green is for your father's eyes," my mom had said, her own blue eyes sparkling. "And the star in the circle is a symbol of a witch, where your dad comes from."

Where dad came from. They both had told me stories ever since I was little, about the land they called, "where Daddy came from." Dad talked about it so much he seemed to like that world better than this one. I never really believed the stories he told me about falling through a magical portal and arriving in a brand new world, completely different from his own. I just figured it was a story he told to keep me entertained.

I opened the cover of the book and irritably flipped through the pages. There was just page after page of blank paper. It was a family tradition to keep a journal. Aunt Bella, Uncle Chase, and Dad himself had done it. I knew because I had seen the journals on the top shelf of our library. Every once in awhile, the thought crossed my mind to read them to see if what he told me was true, but I never did.

I glanced at my blank journal. The idea that I could write something memorable was laughable. I heard footsteps coming down the stairs, and I quickly shoved the journal back into my school bag. If he saw me even looking at it, he would get his hopes up.

My dad came down the stairs. He was quite tall with windswept golden-blonde hair, pale skin with a sprinkling of freckles, and startling green eyes. He was wearing a long-sleeved blue shirt with a crooked green-striped tie. His belt was half fastened to a pair of brown pants.

"Dad, you look like you're trying to make a better impression than I am." I was wearing a plain white shirt and blue pants with black shoes. My brown hair, which was slightly long, was in a single braid down my back.

"Well, I'm your dad, I'm supposed to look impressive." He finished fastening his belt. "We're late."

"I don't care."

He gave me a fatherly glare as he bent down to tie his shoe. "You'll like the school. It's run by Jasper's son, remember?"

"I remember." Jasper had been his teacher when he first really began learning magic when he turned sixteen.

He ran into the kitchen and came back with my lunch. "Come on, get up. We need to get going."

"Where's Mom?"

"She's coming." He glanced at his watch.

My mother glided down the stairs in this beautiful springlike yellow dress. Her hair was in a bun, and she had light pink lipstick on. Her skin was pale and seemed to glow, and she had dark brown hair exactly like mine. I was secretly jealous of my mother's beauty. She always looked like a goddess no matter if it was the morning and she'd just gotten out of bed, or if she hadn't put makeup on yet.

"I'm ready," she said as she kissed him on the cheek. She turned to me. "Are you ready, sweetie?"

I nodded.

"She doesn't want to go," Dad said, leading the way out the door. I followed, and my mother came after me, shutting the door behind her.

"You'll do fine," she said as we walked down the lawn. "Everyone is nervous on their first day."

"I know." My stomach was still in a knot.

"You'll be home by 3:30. Then we can have dinner and help you with your homework."

She made it sound so simple. There was still making friends and seating arrangements. I had to meet teachers, and then there was the fact that I wouldn't do any of my homework. I wasn't as perfect as my parents liked to believe.

"Why can't I go to boarding school?"

"Oh, so you believe I came here and went to a boarding school with your mom just as I've always said I have?"

"No, I know that's part of your made-up story."

My parents exchanged glances and I rolled my eyes.

"Are you trying to get rid of us?" A mocking smile lingered on my mom's lips.

I scowled. "No."

"I think she answered that too quickly, Charlotte," Dad said with a smirk.

"So do I."

"Ugh!" I marched ahead of them on the dirt road and heard them laughing. My cheeks burned. When were they ever going to give these stories up? They always made fun of me and laughed when I disbelieved their fantasies. It wasn't as if I didn't believe there were other worlds out there. In school, they taught us that ours wasn't the only place with magic, that there were other worlds, dimensions out there some with magic, some without. I just didn't think my dad came from another one. He was so normal, so average compared to everyone here. He was the best at any magic there was. How could he come from some place that didn't have magic?

Dad caught up with me. "I'm sorry Rose. I just like how stubborn you are. You're so like your mother."

I sighed. "I just want to get this day over with."

"It will be. Soon."

We could see the school now from where we walked. My face twisted, nervousness taking over.

"You'll do fine," he said, pulling me into a much-needed but surprising hug. "Everything is going to go smoothly."

We walked up to the school's entrance. It was so tall, it

looked like it might crush us. It was at least three stories and made of old crumbling brick and the windows were made of thick, iridescent glass. At the top of the gargantuan structure was a pointed roof. I dizzily wondered how many classrooms could fit in a school that high. The walls were made of a muddy looking brick. I glanced back at the thick glass windows. They didn't seem like you could see anything from the inside.

After meeting with the principal, who gave me and about ten other new students our schedules, I started out my day. I would have five classes a day, a packed schedule, starting the day with Basic Magical History. History was interesting enough, but there were still more doodles in my notebook than notes.

In each of my classes, we were kept within our age bracket. Since I was sixteen, I was in classes that had fifteen and sixteen year olds. I didn't have the same people in every class, thank goodness. There were boys who flirted with the good-looking girls, and also several girls who had nothing better to do than gossip.

The second to last class of the day was Magic Concepts, which started right away with learning how to develop power stones. It seemed strange to me to start off with something so big, but I had always wanted to know how to make one.

Power Stones: An object, most commonly a stone, that contains a person's magical essence. Containing a person's magical powers, it becomes the source. If the stone is broken, a person's powers can disappear along with it.

The reading felt dry and it made me impatient to start making power stones. I had waited so long to start, and all we were doing was reading about them. Besides all that, I wouldn't have any powers to put in a power stone. Nothing had shown up yet. I sighed heavily and turned the page.

By the end of the day I was ready to go home. We'd already been given homework, which really put me in a grumpy mood. I was in my last class of the day, about basic magic. In a few months, we would learn how to make our own wands and then get our power stones. Hopefully in a few months I would have something to show for it.

I was sitting at the back of the class; if I took out

something, the teacher wouldn't notice. Trying to be quiet, I took out my blank journal, turned to the first page and started drawing a flower. I was halfway through drawing the petals when someone tapped me on the shoulder. Thinking it was the teacher, I jumped, and turned around.

It was the girl sitting behind me. She had a kind face, small and narrow. She had very pale skin considering we were coming from one of the hottest summers we'd had in the past three years. Her eyes were brown, and her black hair was so long, silky, and curly it made me feel a small twinge of jealousy. That was strange, because I'd never felt jealous over a fellow student's looks before. Her hair fell down her back like waves, just the tips of them curled.

She waved at me and pointed to my drawing.

"What?" I mouthed. I glanced at the teacher. He had his back turned, writing something on the chalkboard.

The girl pointed again. I handed the notebook and pencil back to her. She scribbled for a minute and then handed it back to me.

I like your flower. Where did you learn to draw like that?

Not only was I jealous of her hair, I was jealous of her handwriting. I wrote back.

Thanks. It's a rose. My mom taught me to draw it because "Rose" is my name.

Nice name. I'm Jasmine. I'm in 2 of your classes.

What classes? I was curious now.

Archery and this class, I think.

Archery! I remembered her now. Every time she had been called to shoot she'd hit the target. Everyone was envious of her. Well, the boys were more in love with her than jealous. The first day and she already had our class wrapped around her finger.

I remember. You hit the target every time you were called up. Nice job.

She smiled as she read my note.

Thanks. I just practice a lot. It's one of my favorite things to do.

My dad is really good at archery. He was at the top of his class when he was in school.

"Ladies, what are you doing?" the teacher asked.

I turned back around in my seat, taking the notebook out

of Jasmine's hands. "Just checking to see if my notes are correct, sir," I said.

I could hear Jasmine trying to hold back laughter as the teacher nodded and turned back to the board.

When the bell finally rang, I turned to Jasmine. "That was fun," I said, grinning.

"Especially because we got away with it." She winked at me as we walked out of the class together. I giggled.

We walked out into the afternoon together, leaving the school behind us.

"Do you have any homework?" Jasmine asked.

"Yeah." I didn't want to think about it. "I'm probably going to wait till the last minute."

"Same," she said, running her hand through her beautiful black hair. "I really hate homework."

We walked together, our feet keeping beat with each other.

"Your first day was really impressive," I said. "You're the best in all your classes and all the boys are head-over-heels in love with you."

She threw back her head and laughed. "If they knew why they were in love with me, they wouldn't be so keen on it."

"What, are you some seductive sorceress or something?"

"Something like that, yes."

We walked in silence for a minute. I listened to the rhythm of our feet together. I broke the pleasant silence when we reached the road leading to my house.

"Do you want to come for dinner? My parents would be very happy to see I made a friend on my first day. I wasn't happy about going this morning."

"I would love to, but I can't," she apologized. "At my house dinner is a family affair. I can't skip out on it."

"Oh. Okay then. I'll see you tomorrow." To my surprise, I was looking forward to it.

"See you." We waved and parted ways, Jasmine headed toward the woods.

Watching her go, I smiled to myself. I'd already made a friend who had changed my attitude toward school, but she had not changed my attitude toward homework.

Chapter 2: Secrets

When I got home, the house was empty and quiet. As I shut the door, the cool September air nipped at my skin, not quite wanting to let me go. Both my parents worked, so I wasn't worried, they'd be home soon enough. Skipping up the stairs two at a time, I ran to our room we called the "Little Library."

When my parents had moved in, the house had three bedrooms. After I was born, they turned the smallest bedroom into a library. It was my favorite room in the house. There was a window with a beautiful view and a window seat, nestled between two bookshelves. My favorite thing to do was sit in the window seat and read, hiding the books I was reading under the seat.

I lifted the window seat lid and took out the book I currently had hidden there, but found I didn't want to read it. I was restless and bored. Sometimes even a book couldn't remedy that. At the top shelf of the bookcase on the door's left hand side, were four of my father's journals from his youth, sitting there patiently. He wouldn't be home for a while yet. I had plenty of time to read them and put them back on the shelves.

I glanced down at my book again. Was that right? Journals were places to record your private thoughts—something I had a hard time comprehending—but reading someone else's journal might mean absolute betrayal. But these were the journals of his teenaged years. Would my father even care? Slowly, I got up and retrieved the first journal from its place on the shelf.

I opened the cover; it was stiff with disuse. I felt afraid my dad was going to suddenly be at the window, but nothing was there except our normal, quiet backyard. I turned back to the journal and began to read the first entry: *Summer is coming....*

After a few minutes, I was able to relax and read with ease. Dad had a very organized mind, very calm and collected for a kid my age. However, I could tell there was this wild part of him just yearning to reach out and test himself. Time seemed suspended in my own world as time in his world began to speed up. Years passed. He met my mother, whom he went to school with, and met his friends. A few years after he'd been in this world for a while, he went back to his. He became depressed and withdrawn, his entries short and bitter. One night, his sister, my Aunt Bella, followed him, finding the entrance to this world. In the process, she found out about her brother's secret second life.

Then as he was getting older, things started getting more serious.

I started learning how to make power stones today. It's hard to imagine all your magic power trapped in one small stone. Everyone has one as a bracelet, or a necklace. It's what makes your power the strongest, containing it in a natural object, like a stone. If it ever broke...all my magic would be gone, possibly forever. Is it worth the gamble, to make myself more powerful?

Andrew

As I kept reading, I found something that surprised me. It was toward the end of his last journal, when all the danger and war was over and things were just getting back to normal.

Last night was...exquisite. Even that is not enough to describe how I felt. It was a kind of closure. Charlotte told me she felt the same way. After the loss of her parents, she needed anything to help her through this hard time, the hard aftermath of everything that's happened. Last night is exactly what both of us needed.

Andrew

I read the entry over again, trying to look between the lines. Charlotte was my mother's name. If he had been dating her since he was eighteen, they must have been together longer than I thought. What were they doing the night he described as "exquisite"? I couldn't ask, because that would mean confessing I'd read his journal. I continued reading. In about ten pages, a few months had passed. There was a super-short entry halfway down the middle of one page.

Charlotte hasn't been feeling very well for a while. This morning when she threw up after breakfast, I suggested she go to the doctor. When she came back she told me the news: she's pregnant.

Andrew

I sat staring at the little open book. How could he have been so stupid? How could my mom have been so stupid, to have a kid that early on in life? Then I caught myself. If that hadn't happened, I wouldn't exist.

That was messed up.

I heard the key turn in the lock. I quickly untangled myself from my reading corner, and raced to put away the journals. My mind was cluttered with panic, but hopefully my dad wouldn't be able to tell what I was doing.

However, he must've heard my footsteps, because he called, "Rose?" as he hung up his coat.

"I'm upstairs reading!" I called. I rushed down the stairs, picking a random book off the shelves to add to my charade.

The next morning, I hurried out the door, declining his offer to walk me to school before he had to go to work. I was too freaked out by what I read in his journals to talk to him at the moment. I kept busy with the things I needed to do so he would think I was stressed.

To my surprise and relief Jasmine was waiting for me at the end of my road. She was lying in the grass despite the icy morning dew.

"Jasmine?"

When she heard my voice, she opened her eyes and sprang gracefully to her feet.

"Hi, Rose! I hope you don't mind me waiting for you."

"I don't mind at all." We began walking. She must have seen the nervous look on my face.

"Are you alright?"

"Just a late night is all. I read my dad's journals from when he was my age."

She raised her eyebrows, a half smile on her lips. "Does he know you read them?"

"I'm trying to keep that from him," I mumbled. "I just can't get something out of my head."

"Anything interesting?"

"He wrote about my mom's pregnancy."

"That must have been strange for you to read about."

"Yeah."

A wind stirred and blew our hair around. I zipped up my jacket tighter. We continued to walk, bags and feet keeping a beat.

"Did you do your homework last night?" asked Jasmine.

Damn! "I completely forgot about it!"

She laughed shortly. "It's okay. It's only the first day. I'm sure they'll let you off the hook."

"I hope you're right."

But my high hopes were beaten down. I wasn't given a bad grade, but all the teachers who had given me homework told me it was due tomorrow morning before class. They also added on the homework everyone else got as a bonus. By the end of the day, I was in a bad mood, and was happy I had Jasmine to walk me home.

I knew better than to think the homework would do itself. I did it as soon as I got home, on the floor of the Little Library. I had a writing assignment, describing what experience in magic I'd already had. It felt like a tedious waste of time, and it didn't help with my penmanship skills, but I did it anyway, dating it and writing my name at the top.

Rose King, September 2nd

Exposure to Magic

My parents are very responsible people. They've made sure that I've had some exposure to magic, so when I got to school, I wouldn't be completely in the dark. They taught me the Original Magic the best they could as I was growing up. My dad is talented at the Original Magic and can also read minds. While I don't have many powers yet, I've developed a few like Telekinesis. That's very useful when you don't want to get up and get something.

It wasn't my best work, but I felt like it would satisfy my teacher. I shut the notebook and stuffed it back in my bag. I took out my history book. We were supposed to read chapter two and take notes, but I hadn't even opened to the first page yet. I took out my notebook and began scribbling, wishing more than ever that my handwriting looked like Jasmine's.

During the next two weeks, it became habit for Jasmine to wait for me so we could walk to school and walk home together after. We always parted at the same place. I would head down my road and she'd go off towards the woods. Once or twice I considered following her, but thought better of it. In the few weeks I'd gotten to know her, I knew she had sly cunning, and would probably figure out that I was following her before I could get far.

That's why I wasn't surprised to find her waiting for me one morning in October. She was sitting cross-legged on the ground. She had an orange leaf in her hair and was twirling a red one between her fingers. I also noticed something else: she had cut her hair shorter and dyed the tips of the curls a bright, sky blue.

"Hey!" I called, waving. She smiled, getting to her feet.

"I like your hair. My parents would never let me dye mine."

She laughed in her enchanting way and put the leaf she was holding into my hair, tucking the stem behind my ear.

"I just did it on a whim." She was incredible off-hand. "My parents didn't mind because it only lasts about six weeks."

"In my family that would be about six weeks too many." Laughing, we began walking to school.

"What are you dressing up as for Halloween?" I asked. "It's only a week away."

"A vampire," she said, and grinned.

I laughed as I thought of my Aunt Wendy. She was a vampire.

"What's so funny?" she demanded.

"I just know a vampire."

She raised her eyebrows. "Really, how so?"

"I call her Aunt Wendy. She's a close friend of the family. She's married to a vampire named Jack. They were husband and wife as humans, back in the early 1700s."

"They sound pretty interesting."

"There's never a dull moment."

Jasmine was quiet.

"Hey, do you want to come over to my house this afternoon?" I asked, to cheer her up. "We can do homework together. You can make sure I don't skip out on my work."

"Your parents are okay with it?"

"I asked them if I could invite you."

"Alright, I just can't stay for dinner."

"Right."

I was happy with my success as we continued walking

toward the school. I felt as if I had just caught the elusive and manipulative Jasmine by a snare, and I wasn't about to let go.

That afternoon, Jasmine and I were in the middle of doing history reports when my dad knocked on the library door.

"Rose, do you have a minute? A letter just came for you from Wendy and Jack."

"A letter!" How strange it was to get a letter from them right after I told Jasmine who they were. I took it from him. "Thanks."

"Let me know what they are up to." He left, closing the door behind him.

"Read it out loud," Jasmine said.

"Okay." I ripped open the envelope.

Wendy had written the letter this time. I began reading.

Dear Rose,

Everything is going fine. We've just arrived in the city of Neyoka. We'll be staying here for two months. We are staying at a nice hotel that is comfortable, and we're happy. Once spring rolls around we are planning a trip to come and see you and all our old friends. Hope you are doing well.

Wendy and Jack

Jasmine continued staring at the letter when I finished. "She has the same handwriting as me," she whispered.

"Oh, yeah. That's cool, I never noticed that."

Jasmine continued staring.

"Are you okay, Jasmine?"

"Yeah. I'm fine. Yes."

I gave her a look. "Are you sure? Is something wrong?"

"No, nothing is wrong. I just thought it was weird that we have almost the exact same handwriting. Let's get back to studying."

"I want to write a letter back to Wendy."

"You can do that after," she said, tapping her pencil on her notebook repeatedly, avoiding my eye. "Come on, we need to focus."

"Fine." I put the letter inside a notebook in my backpack, and returned back to my report.

Later, when Jasmine went home, I had time to write a

letter back. I took out a blank piece of paper.

> *Dear Wendy and Jack,*
> *It was good to hear from you! I'm glad everything is going well. Things are going fine here. School has started. I'm not too fond of the homework, but I made a new friend who helps me keep on track. My parents are both doing well at their jobs and get the weekends off. It's getting cold— winter is on the way. Can't wait to see you in the spring!*
> *Love,*
> *Rose*

I sat down on my bed and lay on my back. Why had Jasmine been so evasive? Did she know Wendy and didn't want to tell me for some reason? Was she afraid of vampires? I rolled onto my stomach and sealed the letter in an envelope, writing the address, and marched downstairs.

Whatever it was, I would find out.

The next day, Jasmine and I had an argument. Maybe it was because of my rising suspicion that she was lying to me. Maybe it was because I didn't trust her. But when it came, it exploded, not leaving us on good terms.

I invited her over to my house for lunch, with half a mind to question her. When she arrived I was lying on my bed, staring at the ceiling, and when she opened the door I didn't react.

"Rose?"

I just blinked at the ceiling, waiting for her to care more.

She shut the door. "Is something wrong?"

"Yeah." I sat up and put my right hand to my forehead in anticipation of the head rush. "I want to know why you've been acting so weird lately."

"I don't know what you're talking about."

"Evasive. Lying. Avoiding me. You know exactly what I'm talking about."

She looked down at her feet. "Rose, we're still getting to know each other. I'm not going to tell you everything."

"There was nothing shocking about that letter from Wendy, and yet you acted like you'd seen a ghost."

That got her attention. Her head snapped up, and there was a certain meanness in her eyes. "You're pen-pals with a vampire, Rose. There is 'something shocking' in that, I would have to say."

Her words set me back on my heels. "Were you ever hurt by a vampire?" I hadn't considered that the situation might be personal to her. Maybe I was pushing the limits.

"Who hasn't been hurt by one of them?" she muttered, looking away from me. "They kill people."

"Wendy doesn't."

"And how was I supposed to know that?"

"You're right," I said, "I'm sorry."

She looked away from me, the anger still settling in her eyes. A few minutes passed in silence before I broke it.

"Hey," I said gently, reaching for her arm. "I really am sorry."

"And that means I'm automatically supposed to forgive you? You really need to consider other people's feelings before you go picking fights." The hate was back in her eyes as she stared at me. I looked away, ashamed, as she marched out the door.

The next few days felt pointless without her in them. I had gotten so used to her being there with me, spending the day with her, that everything just felt blank. She was the first real friend I'd ever had, and now that she was gone I didn't know what to do.

Until I found her drinking hot chocolate in my living room one day in mid December.

I was so shocked I dropped my bag. "What are you doing here?"

"Well hello to you too," she said, smiling at me. Her lips were stained with chocolate that she licked off as we stared at each other.

Dad came into the room. "Oh, hi, honey," he said to me, patting me on the shoulder as he passed me. "She wants to talk to you," he whispered in my ear. "And I think it's a good idea, you haven't been talking for long enough."

Like I couldn't tell she wanted to talk to me with her right here in my living room. Thanks, Dad.

He left to go drink coffee and read in his room, and I was alone in the living room with silence stretching between me and Jasmine.

She put down her drink. "Rose...."

"Not here," I said. "In the library."

"Why the library?"

"My dad could clearly over hear us here."

She followed me up the stairs, and the only sound was our feet on the carpeted steps.

The feel of the room, of the pages promising stories and information made me more relaxed. I took a deep breath, and then turned around to face my best friend.

"What has been going on with you?" I demanded.

She just stared at me.

"Come on, spit it out!" My voice was rising. "If our friendship is going to work, you can't keep lying when I ask you questions. If you don't want to answer them, okay, whatever, but don't lie. How can I trust you if I don't know what to believe what comes out of your mouth?"

"Rose."

"What?"

"I'm a vampire."

The silence was instant. My mind went blank. Had my dad tried to read my mind at that moment, it would've been a literal blank, white nothingness.

I turned and sat at the window seat looking out over my front lawn. I wasn't frightened of her, I wasn't in shock. I was letting my mind wander. Drift away from me, away from my body and up into the sky. When I looked at her again, she was gazing at me the same way I'd just been gazing at the sky.

"How are you feeling?" she asked in a gentle, silky voice.

"I feel fine," I said. "You forget, I have an aunt and uncle who are vampires. If you wanted me to be frightened, you're going to be disappointed."

"I don't want you to be frightened." I expected her to smile or laugh, but she didn't do anything. Her face was as straight and as serious as I'd ever seen it.

She came closer, kneeling down in front of me, putting her

pale hand on my arm.

"I'm still Jasmine. Rose, I'm so, so sorry. I wouldn't have kept it a secret, except I had no idea how you would respond."

"No, it's alright," I said. "I wasn't expecting it, but I get it. You didn't want to lose me." I squeezed her hand back and noticed for the first time how different our skin tones were. My hand was shaking just slightly.

She nodded and exhaled. I could almost see the weight of the secret lift off her shoulders.

I no longer felt that strange unease. She was my friend again—Jasmine, the vampire.

The silence lasted a few seconds, and then I asked, "How old are you?"

She smiled. "I'm not sure you want to know that."

"What are you doing in school?"

"Humans are so interesting." She tucked her hair behind her ears and it was just then that I noticed how dark her eyes were. "I became a vampire at sixteen. I'm never going to get older, so might as well blend in. Besides, I don't know any other vampires. It gets lonely."

"So you don't have parents?" I asked, and her face fell.

"I searched for them, once. But they must have been human, I never found any trace of their existence." She was looking down at her lap, and I thought she might cry.

I leaned forward and hugged her. "You're not alone anymore," I said.

The next day, getting ready for school, my stomach was full of knots. My hands were shaking as I put on my coat. Relax, I thought. She's still Jasmine.

"Do you want me to come with you?" Dad asked as I grabbed an apple for breakfast and was walking out the door. Jasmine had told him her secret, because she knew it would be impossible for me to keep it off my mind, and it would be impossible for him not to listen.

"She's still Jasmine," I said without looking at him, turning my back and shutting the door. I took a deep breath before I stepped off the porch, ashamed of myself. I really needed to work on becoming a better daughter.

She was waiting for me, like always, at the corner of the road. Her bag was slung over her shoulder and she was faced away from me. Her black, blue tipped hair moved with the icy wind.

"Hey," I said. I reached into my pocket, my fingers seeking out a small golden dragon figurine my dad had given me when I was six years old. I'd named him Teddy, and to this day, I almost never left the house without putting him in my pocket.

She turned and smiled. As we looked at each other, I realized nothing needed to be said or done. It had all happened last night.

She began walking away, and I matched pace with her until we reached the school. We only said one thing before we went our separate ways.

"Still friends?" she asked.

"Still friends," I said.

Part 2

Chapter 3: Children in Rags

School got harder as the year went on, and sometimes it seemed as if the only thing that brought me peace was my friendship with Jasmine. I could talk to her about the teachers I hated, and we could joke about burning our homework together. It didn't matter that she was a vampire. She seemed to be telling the truth about not hurting people, and I believed her.

"I was all alone," she told me once. "It seemed unfair that I should kill someone and take them away from someone else, someone who could be their whole world. I never found out who turned me," she told me, her eyes darkening. "Better for him, anyway, because if I ever found him, I would rip his throat out."

Our friendship was pretty much the same, except I stopped inviting her to dinner. She didn't tell me what she did when she disappeared into the woods, and I didn't ask. Sometimes even in friendships there are secrets.

As December became late January, I was constantly reminded of how much I hated my teachers, and which ones I hated most. I was never that good at writing (something I was constantly reminded of because my father's old journals sat in our library at home) and I had a teacher that made us write something everyday.

Prompt: Do you have an individual power? What is it?

My answer: Nope.

Prompt: Is there something about yourself that makes you feel good?

My Answer: No. School is bad and I have no powers. Dad can read minds, but I can't. What is wrong with me???

One time, my teacher pulled me aside (her name was Ms. Perk, of all things). She had my journal on her lap, her pointer finger slowly tapping the cover, her face lined with concern. "Rose, I'm concerned about some things I've been reading in your journals."

She waited, but I didn't say anything.

"Rose, just because you don't have a power doesn't mean

there's something wrong with you. Plenty of people who don't have powers of their own can still learn the Original Magic. Nothing is wrong with that."

"My dad can read minds," I mumbled.

"And that power didn't turn up until his late teens, if I remember correctly. His name is quite famous around here. He turned out just fine."

I just looked away, trying my hardest not to cry.

She waited again, but when I didn't say anything, she sighed. "Now run along. You're late for your next class."

Great. She left me feeling like I had to live up to some family legacy now. I was already failing.

When I got home after school, the house was quiet. I checked the clock in the living room. My parents wouldn't be home for another half hour.

I got wood for the fireplace, stacking the kindling and logs against each other. I worked efficiently, my mind blank. When I stuffed as much paper in between the wood as I could, I lit a match, throwing the whole thing onto the pile of tinder.

It caught in a flash, and sparks of orange ate up the paper in seconds. I quickly opened my school bag and took out the damn journal I had to write in everyday. I tore out my September 5th entry, September 6th, and September 7th, throwing them into the fire. They burned away like the early days never existed. It wasn't until I got to the mid-November entries that I threw the whole notebook into the fire, then sat back to watch it burn.

It wasn't until I sat back that I felt the tears on my face.

As the fire grew larger, sweat beaded on my face. I wiped at it, and the sweat mixed with the tears until I stopped and just sat there sobbing.

Then when the clock rang in the half hour, I ran.

Even though it was late January, the sun was out as I ran deeper and deeper into the woods. The light warmed my back and cleared my mind of all the thoughts that had been jumping around and refusing to be quiet for the past few days. My only thought was getting away from all the reminders of what a failure

I was.

I thought maybe if I sat alone in the forest for a while and calmed myself, things would get better. If I could just stop myself from thinking for a little while, maybe this would all blow over, and I could go back to school the next day confidently. I could ask Dad to teach me something. Maybe he knew things the teachers didn't.

I'd stopped in a slight clearing. There were less trees here, and there was evidence of animal tracks when I looked at the snow. Deer and rabbit prints criss-crossed each other, sparkling like crystal in the playful sunlight.

A slight breeze rustled my hair. Taking a deep breath, my lips curled into a smile as I drifted down to the ground like a fallen feather. I forced my eyes to stay closed. I wouldn't look yet; it wasn't time. I didn't feel completely alone, I just felt cold.

But then the earth changed to absorb my impact; shifted, forming to fit my body. It was hot, burning the back of my neck, the only bare skin on my body exposed to the naked ground. I could hear different sounds now: a steady soft crashing, and the scent of salt on the air.

I slowly opened my eyes.

The ground shifted under me as I sat up, and I realized I was sitting on hot sand. I was on a beach. I could hear seagulls crying overhead and the soft crashing was the sound of salt waves.

Had I fallen asleep? I felt no fogginess, no confusion. I could actually feel the sand when I stood up and stumbled toward the waves. It was hard to feel temperature, or true texture, in dreams. The waves almost reached my feet, crashing on the shore and then reaching out, stretching to reach me, to soak me in salty water. I skipped away, jumping for joy over what I'd just done.

I had world jumped! So I did have a power! I had heard of the power of visiting different worlds, but I never knew someone that could. I knew this was a different world. I could feel the energy radiating from everywhere: the ground, the waves, and the sky. The power of this place was overwhelming. This world pulsed with energy, a vibrating power that hummed through my body. It warned me that things were going to be different and dangerous, and it also filled me with anticipation.

I ran to the waves as they crashed down and turned into foam, the cold water lapping my ankles and making me gasp. It was so cold. I reached down and let my fingers dangle in the water as the ocean dragged itself back out. I was so giddy I half expected the water to do something bizarre like change color, but of course it didn't. I sank deeper into the ground as the sand was taken out with the water. I didn't even care that my shoes were going to have as much sand as a sandbar. I was still marveling that I'd finally managed to world jump, when a long shadow loomed over me.

It was long and narrow with a wingspan of about fourteen feet. I whipped around, looked up, and nearly screamed.

It was a girl. She was staring at me from about twenty feet up, getting ready to land. She had long, windswept, honey-colored hair getting tangled in the wind and large blue eyes looking right at me.

I stumbled back, more alarmed that she had wings and was flying than her sudden appearance.

She landed just as the water was dragging out, looking at me curiously, her long honey hair falling over one side of her face.

"Who...." I began.

"Look out!" the girl called.

And that's when the wave hit me. This bizarre stranger had me so startled that I hadn't been paying attention to the waves. They smacked me in the back with force that stung. Then I was under water, holding my breath and struggling for the surface, fighting a losing battle as the wave tumbled toward the shore.

Strong hands grabbed my upper arms and pulled me from the water. I broke through the surface, feeling the flying girl's strong arms supporting me, and the bitter taste of saltwater in my mouth.

The girl walked me away from the shore, where the tide couldn't reach, and sat me down on the hot sand, which stuck to my pants.

"Are you okay?" The girl asked, taking her hands off my shoulders.

Coughing, I nodded my answer.

"It's more the shock that gets you than anything else," she said. It took me a minute to realize she was talking about being taken under by the waves, and not about her wings. She was wearing ripped jeans covered in dirt and a long-sleeved orange shirt that was torn around the sleeves. She had no shoes.

"Who are you?" I finally asked when I'd stopped coughing and was wringing my hair out and emptying my shoes of gloppy, brown stand.

"I'm Alice." Her voice was full of confidence and pride, as if nothing could make her more proud than her own name.

"How—why do you have wings?"

She looked confused, as if I was the one who had just landed from the sky.

"You're not from here, are you?"

"Is it that obvious?"

"Kind of. People having wings are not uncommon here."

"I'm a world jumper. Where I come from, that is not normal." I wasn't worried about her thinking I was crazy. A world where a flying girl was regarded as normal, would not consider world jumping strange.

"And this is your first time, isn't it?" Alice asked.

"How did you guess that?"

"World jumpers are often oblivious to new changes, such as a flying girl." She gestured at herself, and I noticed her wings were a very light brown, matching her hair. The feathers were ruffled and spread out behind her.

"Yeah, this is my first time," I confessed. I still couldn't help glowing with pride at my new talent.

"If you were surprised by me, you're going to be surprised a lot." She grinned.

I smiled; I couldn't help it. Alice was different, even aside from the giant brown wings.

"I'm not planning on staying that long."

"Well, you shouldn't just disappear!" she protested. "You should come meet my family!" She jumped to her feet, holding out her hand, her wings limp against her back.

"Isn't that a little sudden?" I asked, glancing at her hand, suspicions running through my mind.

"Well, when you world jump you have to see the places you go. Come on."

I wanted to give in to the ache inside me that yearned to see this new world; but was it safe? Cautiously, I took her hand, and began walking down the beach.

Alice walked with a spring in her step and a smile on her face. She gave off a strong vibe of independence, pride, and fierceness that didn't make me want to stand too close to her. Whatever this girl was up to, she wasn't kidnapping me. She was too honest for that. I didn't think she had even given me a fake name. I wasn't in any danger here. And if at any time I felt as if I was, I could just think of home, and I was confident I would find myself back there.

We walked for a long time, off the beach, over the grassy sand dunes, and into a town. We used the side streets behind buildings and through alleys instead of the main streets. Alice started walking faster and faster; the small stones and broken glass didn't seem to affect her bare feet at all. The buildings were made mostly of gray stone. They were so tall and narrow, they completely casted shadows over the alleys.

There was a horrible odor to the place I couldn't quite identify. It smelled like a mix of waste, rotting food, and sewage. I wrinkled my nose the farther we went into the shanty town. Alice didn't seem bothered by any of it. She kept going, a destination in mind; I walked behind her, almost out of breath, with the strong bad smell bothering me.

I was just about to ask Alice where we were going when I heard music. Alice must've heard it too, because she began walking faster in that direction.

The music got louder as we kept moving and the smell finally cleared. The town was filled with people and we easily blended in with the crowd.

As we entered the center of town the clouds cleared, the sky brightened, and the music sharpened. It was a lone violin, its fast music swept the air and filled the dreary town with lively sound.

A thick crowd surrounded the source of the music. Alice

pushed us to the front.

A tall blonde girl tapped her foot to the music, the bow in her hand flying across a small, intricate violin. Her chin was in the chin rest, her eyes closed as she let her hands do the talking. The notes were so fast and sharp it made me dizzy.

She was wearing a dazzlingly sky-blue dress that flowed as she moved, sparkling as if it had been dipped in the Milky Way. The neck was low cut, but her hair, thick and flowing like the dress, covered the exposed skin.

She finished the song with a few quick notes, and then she bowed. Applause replaced the sound of her music—coins were tossed in her empty violin case.

She looked up at Alice and me with deep-green eyes.

She was very beautiful. She was tall and thin—maybe twenty years old, possibly one or two years younger. She had flowing golden hair. A narrow jaw and fair skin made up her face, along with thin arched eyebrows that framed those startling green eyes.

Not noticing my shocked face, she lifted her violin case and rattled it as the crowd disappeared, money jingling inside.

"Nice going, Lucy!" Alice congratulated her friend.

Lucy smiled, and I found it odd she'd not yet spoken.

Lucy poured the coins into Alice's waiting hands and then put her violin away. I admired the impressive instrument before she closed the case. When I looked up I started, because the beautiful dress she'd been wearing was gone, replaced by a dirty ripped outfit. She was now wearing a short-sleeved lavender shirt streaked with mud and blue shorts that were practically in tatters.

"Yes! Now the others will be happy. Come on, Lucy." Alice grabbed Lucy's hand and ran, calling, "Come on!" As she did, Lucy looked back at me, probably wondering why a stranger was following them around. Still, she didn't speak.

We found our way out of the little city. On the way out they bought bread, cheese, and a very small amount of meat that didn't look particularly edible. We left the city quickly and quietly, leaving all the bad smells and dirty alleys behind.

We walked until the sun started to set into the mountains, making the green trees look like they were on fire. We slipped into the shadows the forest provided and it was so dark that I was nervous all over again.

After five minutes, a light came into view that made me think the forest really was on fire: in the distance a small orange light that flickered like a candle.

"Alice," I said. I stopped, fear making my voice thick.

"It's alright, it's just the gang," Alice said.

"The gang?" I took a step back.

"My family," she said. "Let's go."

My heart pounding, I began following her again. I had heard of gangs. Weapons and violence were only part of it. But Alice seemed like the kind of person who could take on a bloodthirsty gang single-handedly.

We broke through the last bit of trees separating us from the light and the supposed gang that surrounded it.

All I saw when we arrived in the clearing were four kids: three boys and one girl who looked as dirty and ragged as Alice did.

A tall, thin girl with black hair shading her eyes, pale skin, and wearing a dirty black shirt, and ripped black jeans was lying against a boy's chest. She looked up with lazy eyes. When she saw me, her eyes went wide and she bolted upright.

"Alice, what did you do?"

"This is...." Alice looked at me for the first time since we entered the woods. "I realized I never caught your name."

"Emily," I said quickly, thinking fast. Alice may trust me enough to give me her real name, but I wasn't as trusting.

The next oldest boy had blonde hair and blue eyes, and he was sitting next to the boy who had been sitting with the girl in black. His eyes shined as he looked at me, a smile curling up his lips, which made me even more nervous.

"This is Emily," Alice was saying. My eyes darted back to the girl in black. "I found her on the beach."

"You found her on the beach," the girl repeated in disbelief.

"Yes," said Alice simply.

"And you didn't think about telling us that?"

"And how would I do that?" Alice argued. "I don't have

telepathy."

"We're supposed to keep ourselves hidden," the girl pointed out.

"Yeah, like going out and performing like monkeys in the streets is keeping ourselves hidden," Alice retorted.

Lucy looked hurt and gave Alice a look. She didn't defend herself by replying.

"You have to send her back," the girl said. She looked at me directly. "You have to go back."

"Bella," said the boy she'd been sitting with. I was shocked this girl had the same name as my Aunt Bella, my dad's sister.

"Well, what are we supposed to do with her?" asked Bella, insultingly irritated, as if I were an unwanted item they wanted to return to the store.

"I'm just passing through," I said, the note of defense clear in my voice. "Alice saved me from drowning."

Alice was grinning, obviously enjoying my exaggeration. Bella looked shocked, and out of the corner of my eye, I saw the blonde boy smile.

"She did?" Bella asked.

"I don't just bring random strangers into our group," Alice said. "I have a reason for everything I do."

Lucy raised her eyebrows, and kindness replaced the fierce look on Bella's face. "Alright then, you can stay," she said. "I'm sorry for giving you a hard time."

"It's alright, and thank you." Alice was already sitting on the ground and patted the space beside her. I crossed my legs and sat down.

The fire crackled and popped. I watched the wood turn into embers.

"Oh, I almost forgot!" Alice's voice startled me. "I have food!"

This seemed to be the magic words. Everyone around the circle sat up straighter, and the dull, sleepy looks in their eyes were replaced by ravenous glints. Alice brought out the bread, cheese and meat. Getting to his feet quietly, the blonde boy took a knife from his pocket and began slicing the bread. He divided everything up evenly, giving everyone a share with me last, and there was still more afterwards. Alice tucked it away in a bag.

Alice was putting her cheese on her bread and then letting it melt over the fire. I copied her.

"Who is that blonde boy?" I asked Alice as I took my bread off the fire. The bottom was like toast as I bit into it.

"That's Lucide. He's sixteen, and second in command."

"I take it Bella is leader," I said dryly.

"She is. But don't get too worried about her. She just gets grumpy when she's under a lot of stress."

"What's putting her under stress?"

"Well...that's hard to explain."

I let the subject drop and continued eating.

I would have to leave tonight when they were all sleeping. I'd world jump back to my world and not bother them again. Bella was right; Alice shouldn't have brought me here. I was just passing through, anyway. There was no need for me to even be a temporary burden to this "gang" that was just trying to survive the night.

When everyone was finished eating they started to settle down to sleep. Bella sat down a little away from the group, and Alice whispered in my ear that she was taking first watch. Nodding, I lay my head down, focusing my thoughts on home: my house, my school, and the smell of the air. I would be home again soon. I couldn't wait to tell Jasmine what I could do.

Chapter 4: The Rags and Riches Gang

The next morning I woke up with the sun in my face and groaned. I really needed to work on my landings. Where had I ended up? I turned over and almost screamed. I was still lying next to Alice on the ground in the clearing by the fire. She was asleep, lightly snoring.

My head spun when I sat up, and not just from a head rush.

I was still here. But how was that possible? I had come here just by willing that I be somewhere else, because I didn't have anything in mind. That being said, wouldn't I at least be somewhere else?

My brain was jammed with panic. The only thing I could think of was I had fallen asleep before I could successfully perform the necessary magic. I looked around. The fire had died during the night; all that was left were a few pulsing orange embers. Even Bella was asleep—her thick black hair in tangles as she lay next to the boy in black, who had his hand on her waist. The one on watch now was Lucide, who looked at me when I looked around.

"Morning sunshine," he whispered.

My panic dulled for a second as I looked at his face. It was so calm and smoothed of emotion that I couldn't help but feel calmer.

"Hey," I said going over and sitting next to him. "Are you watch man?"

"For the past hour, since Zorin went to sleep at four."

"Zorin?"

"Bella's boyfriend," Lucide explained, pointing to the boy who had his sleeping hand on Bella's waist.

"Oh." The silence of the sleeping camp was slightly unnerving and reminded me I was alone, and might have failed at returning home. To keep Lucide talking, I asked more questions.

"Who is everyone else in the camp?"

"You've pretty much met everyone," Lucide said. "Alice

and Lucy you've met. Bella is leader, Zorin is her boyfriend and that boy over there..." he pointed to a boy who looked around Zorin's age, who had black hair and tan skin. He was curled up, his knees practically touching his chin, making him seem extremely small, "...is Ginko."

I nodded, my gaze lingering on Ginko.

"So Alice saved you from drowning, did she?"

I shook myself. "Yes, I world jumped and landed in the ocean."

"Were you far out at sea or getting washed up by a wave?"

He was getting a little too curious. I shifted my weight.

"And you have a great name...Emily. How long did it take you to come up with that alias? Two seconds? Or were you thinking about it all the way here?"

"Three seconds, actually," I said, playing along. When he laughed, I said, "How did you know?"

"I have a power that lets me know if a person is lying. If they are, I can tell that they lied more clearly than if they'd confessed to me themselves. I can also control fire. "

"So what's my real name?"

"Sarah?"

"Not even close."

"Merissa?"

"Nope."

"Just tell me."

"I'll give you a clue."

He sighed. "Fine."

"It's a flower name."

"Lily?"

I shook my head. "Rose."

His eyes brightened. "You know what, I like that even better."

My cheeks turned pink.

Lucide stood up and offered me his hand. "Time to wake everyone up."

I took it. "What time is it?"

He glanced at the sun just peeking over the horizon. "Just after five."

"You like to get an early move on, don't you?"

"The early bird gets the worm." He shook Bella's shoulder.

That was the beginning of my first day in a gang. Surprisingly, the problem with going home was pushed to the back of my mind.

When Alice woke I saw her wings were missing.

"What happened to your wings?" I asked.

"They're a spell," she replied. "They only last a few hours." She pulled at a string hanging around her neck. The charm was a small vial filled with golden liquid. She told me once she took a sip, she would have wings for two hours.

Her job every morning was to check on the perimeter of the camp, to make sure there wasn't anyone waiting to ambush them. I began to ask questions and then stopped. It wasn't the time. Still, I wondered what was it about this world that made this little gang so defensive.

"Well, it's time for me to do my job," said Alice, taking a swig from the small vial. She resealed it and let it fall. I watched it swing to a stop on her neck, the liquid that was left sloshing against the smooth glass walls.

She straightened her back as the wings began to grow. It was amazing to watch; at first they were just a silver, blinding light surrounding her back, but then they began to take shape; the silver morphed and shone so brightly for just a few seconds I had to look away. In that short time, her tan-feather-wings were back. The whole transformation took about ten seconds.

"Whoa."

She laughed lightly. "You don't need to be impressed by it. No one else is."

I saw she was right; no one besides me had looked around to watch Alice's transformation. They were all too busy packing up camp.

I looked back at Alice and gave a little shout: she had swooped at me so fast I didn't have time to register it, and then suddenly she was holding me in her strong arms, my feet dangling in the sky, the ground getting farther and farther away by the second. She was holding me firmly by the upper arms, my arms hanging out at an awkward angle.

"Wh...what are you doing?" I asked, breathless and dizzy by the height. Her wings flapped, giving off wind and momentum to go faster and higher.

"Flying, silly, what does it look like?"

"It looks like you're trying to kill me," I gasped.

She laughed again, the sound lost by the wind her wings created. "Now that would be incredibly stupid of me, killing off the Rags and Riches gang's newest member."

"That's what your gang is called?"

"Yep."

"Cool," I approved. And as I said it, the name made more sense. So far, all I'd see them wear were basically rags—clothes so dirty and torn that a washing would be a miracle. And that's when I realized that Lucy's stunning performance dress hadn't been real. It was an illusion created by magic.

"What's up with Lucy?" I finally asked. I was trying to keep my mind off the fact that my legs were dangling in open air. "I mean, why won't she talk?"

"She can't," said Alice, as if the fact was mentioned every day. "She lost her voice a long time ago—none of us know why or how. She can't even remember."

"How does she communicate then? Sign language?"

"No, she has a little notebook she carries with her." She seemed distracted, looking left and right. "Let's land for a minute, my arms are getting tired." She slowed down her speed, which was a relief to my stomach, and we slowly drifted to the ground. We were surrounded by tall trees; as we landed, I saw a few chipmunks and squirrels scurry out of the way.

Alice released my arms, and I leaned against a tree to support my shaking legs. "But anyway," she continued, "sometimes instead of talking to reply, we write our replies, turning it into a little game."

"How old is she?"

"Twenty."

"Then wouldn't she be leader?"

"It'd be hard to be a leader when you have to write down all your orders, don't you think?"

"Yeah, I guess."

Alice craned her neck, looking at our surrounding area. There didn't seem to be anything that concerned her. Even if there was, I don't know how she could see anything; all I saw were green trees.

"What are you looking for?" I asked.

"Let's head back to camp," she said. She grabbed my arms again.

"Please, Alice," I begged. "Can't we just walk?"

She shook her head. "It would take too long." Then she grinned, a reckless look in her eyes. "Don't worry, I won't drop you."

I nodded and squeezed my eyes shut.

"Nothing," she reported to Bella when we landed back in camp five minutes later. "The coast is clear."

"Enjoy the ride, Rose?" Bella asked.

She hadn't used my fake name. Lucide! I turned to glare at him, and he grinned at me.

Bella laughed. "Lucide told us. That was very clever of you."

My cheeks burned, and Alice laughed excitedly, flapping her wings and bouncing like a little child. "There's no point in hiding anything in the Rags and Riches gang."

"That's right," Lucide agreed and winked at me. This time I blushed for a completely different reason.

"We better start going," said Bella. She slipped a backpack over her shoulder and began walking. Zorin matched stride with her, Lucide and Ginko were following them, Lucy was behind them holding her notebook, and then Alice walked with me in the back.

I stared at Lucy's back, questions jamming my brain.

"Go," Alice said when she noticed me staring. "She'll like you."

Taking a deep breath, I walked until I was level with Lucy. "Hi," I said shyly.

Turning to see me, she smiled and waved. I still got a shock from looking at her green eyes. She was waiting for me to say something, and I had no clue what to say.

"Um...Why aren't you the leader?" I could feel myself turning red.

She began scribbling in her notebook and then handed it to me. Feeling embarrassed, I read what she had written.

I was, but I wasn't interested. Bella is a wonderful leader, though.

I smiled and handed her the notebook back. "You played great yesterday. I thought you were amazing."

Thank you, she wrote. *I love playing.*

I smiled at her and then ducked my head. It was hard to talk to her, and I was never very good at conversation. After a few paces, I ended up next to Lucide.

"Is everything okay?" he asked.

"Yes," I said. I peeked at him to see if he caught me in the lie, but he only smiled.

It was around the time things started to wind down for the night that all my worries started coming back. I'd almost forgotten about them. Sharing a life with the Rags and Riches gang was nothing short of complete consumption. I had spent all day helping them out, and by learning what they did, my own worries flew out of my head like birds escaping from a cage. How could I worry about being home in time for dinner when these people might not even have dinner? Spending the day with them made me feel ashamed of myself, but also lucky for what I had.

"Rose?" Alice asked. She was standing in front of me, staring at me curiously. "Dinner time."

"Oh, right," I said. "Thanks." I sat down next to her and folded my hands.

"Where did you go just now?" she asked. "You looked worried."

"Oh, it was nothing," I said. "Just spacing out." I glanced at Lucide, to see if he would sell me out, but he had his head down, over an apple he was slicing. He didn't look at me.

Bella handed me an apple slice and a piece of bread. "I'm sorry the cheese is gone," she apologized.

"That's alright." I took the small meal thankfully as my stomach growled. This was the first thing I'd eaten since the morning. The apple was still crisp as I bit into it and juice flooded my mouth. I tried to eat slowly and let it fill my stomach, but I wasn't anywhere near full when I was done. Zorin, Ginko, and Lucy were all still eating.

I stood up. How could I say goodbye to them? I could hardly thank them for the meal and leave. What was I supposed to do?

I glanced at the fire. It was pretty weak and would need more fuel soon. "I'll get more wood," I said.

Bella was leaning against Zorin's knee. "Thanks Rose," she said, without looking up. She looked like she was about to fall asleep.

"I'll be back," I lied, and retreated into the shadows. I saw Lucide look up. His eyes narrowed before I turned around and walked quickly into the darkness.

I forced myself not to run. I didn't want them to hear me turning my back on them. I tried to think clearly as I walked deeper into the forest. They knew I was only temporary. They couldn't afford to take another person into their group.

I leaned against a tree to rest. I was far enough away that I couldn't even see their fire. That was good. The farther away I was, the less likely it was that I'd think of them when trying to world jump, and so I'd get home safely.

I closed my eyes. I tried to block out my hungry stomach, the smell of smoke and dirt on my clothes. I thought of my parents, my room. The way it felt to sleep in my warm bed, to take a hot shower. I imagined Jasmine's face when she realized I was back.

"What are you doing?"

I jumped. "Lucide!"

"Are we so different that you don't feel you can sleep with us?"

"No!"

He studied my burning face. "I know you're not lying, so what is it?"

"None of your business."

He cocked his head ever so slightly. "Yes, it is."

"No, it isn't. It doesn't involve you."

"Yes it does."

"Go away!"

"No."

"I hate you."

He chuckled darkly. "No, you don't. You're a horrible liar."

"Only around you."

His eyes narrowed as his powers took effect. "You're right about that."

"Of course I am."

"So what are you doing out here?"

I sighed. "I'm trying to go home."

"Without saying goodbye?"

"What was I supposed to say? 'Thanks for the food, sorry to drop in?'"

"You've got a point. But imagine what we would've gone through if you didn't come back, because you said you were going to. We would've gone out searching for you and not gotten any sleep."

"I never thought of that."

"I know you didn't."

"Ugh!"

"What do you really think of us?"

"I can't lie to you, can I?"

"Nope."

"Does Bella plan on keeping me?"

A confused look crossed his face, and then he burst out laughing. "Rose, we haven't kidnapped you!"

"What was I supposed to think?"

"We're just cautious, that's all."

"Cautious! I would call it paranoid."

"Look," he took a step toward me, and I could feel my back pressing up against the tree. "We've been through alot. We just have to make sure we stick together."

"What have you been through?" I whispered. I could smell his sweet breath waff my face as he leaned in.

"Nothing you need to know about yet."

"At least tell me...."

"You can try again in the morning. It's dangerous to world jump at night. Trust me."

"Why...."

"Just trust me. Will you trust me?" he asked, a worried look crossing his face.

I stared at him for a long moment before I heard myself say yes, and it wasn't even a lie.

He pushed off of the tree. "Let's get back."

I followed him out of the forest, feeling confused and scared. If Lucide hadn't interrupted, would my power have worked? I hadn't felt anything, and that scared me.

"We caught a stray wanderer," said Lucide as we arrived back at camp.

I kept my eyes down, and I could feel my cheeks burning.

Bella snorted. "She looks a little too sheepish for a run away."

My eyes snapped up to hers, but she smiled kindly at me. "Welcome back," she said.

I nodded and sat down next to Alice, my face red with shame. Alice affectionately nudged my foot with her toe, and I tried to smile. I didn't know what to say to her.

Later that night at the campfire, Bella sat next to me as I stared into the fire. I ignored her as she sharpened a stick with her knife. If she wanted to earn my respect as some kind of wise leader, she'd have to show me reasons to respect her.

"Lucide told me what happened," she whispered.

I rolled my eyes, but still didn't look at her. "You people can't keep anything secret, can you?"

"Hey, I'm just trying to keep them safe," she said, her tone a little sharper.

"From what? A girl with a flower for a name?" I threw a stone into the fire and sparks flew. It was only then that I realized the camp had become increasingly more quiet.

"What happened back there?"

My throat tightened. "I'm sure Alice has told you by now, but I'm a world jumper. I tried to world jump back home but," I looked her in the eye for the first time. "I couldn't. My power isn't working, and I'm scared. I want to go home."

She looked sympathetic as I explained myself. I hated that look. "Is that good enough for you?" I snapped.

The look in her eyes changed, and of all things, she started to laugh. "You really try to make yourself unlikeable, don't you?"

Chapter 5: A New Member

One night turned into two, and two into three. Each night I tried to get back, and nothing ever worked. They all tried to stay positive for me, but I could see the worry in their eyes. Meanwhile, I was trying to quell my growing panic. There had to be some explanation as to why my powers weren't working. I wasn't practiced enough was the easiest answer, but there had to be something more I was missing.

In the meantime, I learned their routines. They were nomads. They slept in shifts, traveled all day, and when they came across a town, Lucy performed with her violin. Sometimes the others would join in the performance. I learned that the illusion power that had made Lucy's stunning dress was Lucide's. He could make things that seemed real. They would last a few minutes and then fade from existence.

On a good day, we had money left over from buying food, and all of us could pocket some. But we always had to be prepared to give it back, because we never knew when we would get money next. Alice was skilled at stealing, but Bella insisted they keep her robbery skills as a last resort.

One day after I'd been with them for about two weeks, we had it really good. We all had five Nil in our pockets to spend as we pleased. Lucy had played great, and we had eaten well. I went over to congratulate her when Bella came up to me, panicked.

"Have you seen Zorin?" she asked.

"Come to think of it, I haven't," I said, my eyes sweeping the camp—taking in inventory, which was a natural habit to do by now. If we were all together we were safe. Safety in numbers.

"Lucy?" Bella asked.

Lucy shook her head, her hair shading her eyes.

The intensity of the stress got stronger in Bella's eyes.

"Don't worry," I tried to reassure her. "I'm sure he's fine."

"But I'm the leader; I'm supposed to know where everyone is!" Bella practically cried, her voice rising.

I put my hand on her arm. "It's alright, we'll find him."

Turning my head slightly, but keeping my hand on her arm, I spoke to the boys.

"Ginko, Lucide, would you help me look for Zorin?"

"You hold down the fort here with Lucy and Bella," said Lucide, standing up. Ginko jumped to his feet. I nodded. Lucide was second in command; I never questioned his authority.

The two boys disappeared into the trees, and I brought Bella to sit down by the fire. She was so level headed, normally like Lucide. I guess when problems included your boyfriend your perspective changed.

"He didn't tell me where he was going," Bella said, staring at the fire, the light brightening her pale face. "He should have told me where he was going."

"He's very responsible," I said. "He'll be fine."

"If he was responsible he would've told me where he was going," she snapped. "He's in trouble when he gets back."

Lucy smiled, and I leaned over to see what she was scribbling in her notebook.

I'm sure Zorin is fine, but it is never good when Bella Thomson is mad at you.

I smiled. I could imagine that.

Just then we could hear footsteps on the forest floor not far from the camp. We all tensed as a reflex. I saw Bella take out her knife, the silver blade glinting wickedly. I put my hands out, palms flat and forward, in front of my body, as if to brace or block something.

We all stood up, ready for any attack.

But it was Lucide, Ginko, and Zorin. Zorin was in between the two boys, slightly unsteady on his feet.

"Zorin!" Bella cried, running over. "You almost gave me a heart attack. Where have you been?"

Zorin didn't reply, just grinned stupidly.

I went over to the three boys, Lucy behind me. "What's wrong with him?" I asked, my voice urgent.

"I..." Bella seemed at loss for words.

"He's drunk," said Lucide, tightening his grip on Zorin's arm as Zorin swayed slightly.

"Isn't that illegal?"

Lucide shook his head. "In this world the drinking age is sixteen, and Zorin is seventeen."

Zorin burped.

"How much money did he have?" I dug my hand into my pocket and checked for my money, but my five Nil was still there, right next to Teddy. I felt ashamed to have even entertained the thought of Zorin stealing from me; he wasn't an addict.

"He'd been saving up his money for a long time," Lucide replied. "He had twelve Nil. Three Nils a beer, four beers. He was drunk halfway through the third."

Zorin was cross-eyed. He sagged even with Lucide and Ginko supporting him. A throaty chuckle came from his lips.

Bella rolled her eyes. "Zorin, you complete idiot."

"We'll take him to lie down," said Lucide, practically dragging Zorin over by the fire.

"S'not tired," muttered Zorin, his head nodding.

"Oh, yes you are, buddy," said Lucide, patting him on the back and smiling. "When you wake up tomorrow with a hangover, you'll wish you'd gotten more sleep."

"S'my turn to...watch," said Zorin, his eyes closed, barely able to keep his head up.

"I'll take first watch," said Bella savagely. "So I can make sure you never get out of my sight."

"Oh come on Bellie."

"Shut up."

"Those two are going to get married someday," Lucide whispered in my ear. For some reason I blushed. I went to go lie down.

When I'd been lying down for about twenty minutes, Ginko came over and lay down next to me. I smiled at him and went back to star gazing.

"Do you like Lucide?" he asked suddenly.

My head snapped up. "Ginko!" I hissed.

"So you do like him. You immediately assumed I meant attraction instead of just getting along with him." When he saw my mortified look, he smiled. "He's cute. You should go for it."

My blush deepened. "Well, do you like Alice?"

He cleared his throat rather awkwardly. "Um, I'm gay," he

said.

"Oh. Sorry. That's fine. I mean, cool." I looked away from him, embarrassed.

He sat up and smiled, to show me he wasn't offended. "He's not normally my type, but I think he likes you, too."

I nodded distractedly. I did not want to be having this conversation anymore. "What's your power, anyway? I haven't seen you use anything."

"I can create light with my hands, and I'm telekinetic."

I blinked at him, perplexed. "So you're a firefly."

He laughed good-naturedly. "You bet, baby." With this he lifted his left hand and wiggled his fingers. Five pinpoints of light drifted from his fingertips and floated mid air. One tapped me on the nose, and I smiled. I didn't tell him that I hadn't been able to use any of my powers since arriving and I missed using my telekinesis. It was the one thing I was good at.

The pleasant moment was broken by a long, low snore from a passed-out Zorin, sending Ginko and me into a fit of laughter.

I finally felt like I was becoming the newest member of the Rags and Riches gang.

The next morning, I woke up to Alice shaking my shoulder. "Bath time," she said quietly.

I sat up. My hair was a bird's nest. "Wha do ya mean?" I muttered, rubbing my eyes.

Alice snorted. "I thought Zorin was the drunk one. There's a stream nearby. Us girls are going to take a dip. You want to come?"

Standing up, I followed Alice, Lucy, and Bella through the trees.

It was a quiet morning in the forest. Dew was still on the grass, sparkling in rare rays of sunshine. I stumbled on a root, and to my surprise, a tiny fairy appeared out of nowhere and pulled on a lock of my matted hair.

"Hey!" I protested. "Quit it!" I swatted at her, and her golden wings fluttered. I was shocked to realize she was naked.

Bella came over and swatted at the small creature for me.

This time she flew away angrily.

"Do you not have fairies where you're from?" she asked.

"Not angry naked ones," I muttered, and she laughed.

"They don't like seeing humans in the early morning," she explained. "We're too big, and disturb the peace."

I was suddenly aware of a thickness to the air. It seemed this place, this world, had magic threaded in the air, humming with it. I could sense a presence, the sensation close to when you know you're being watched, but the experience was pleasant and uplifting instead of menacing.

"It's so alive here," I said admiringly.

"In some places," Bella sighed. "It's more alive in the woods than anywhere else."

"Why is that?" I asked. We had reached the stream; I could hear the quiet whisper of it just a few yards ahead.

"That's not for you to know," she said, turning away from me.

I stopped walking. I'd had enough of this girl and her evasive answers. My fists tightened. "Why won't anyone tell me what the hell is going on here?"

Bella turned back and cocked her head like a parent amused by an upset child. "Because you're leaving soon, aren't you? I mean, that was your plan, right? I'm not doing this to piss you off, Rose. I'm saving you the nightmares."

I didn't know what to say to that.

Her expression softened. "Race you to the stream?"

I smirked. I obviously wasn't going to get answers today. "I'd like to see you try, Isabella."

And I ran, Bella hot on my heels.

As I hit the water, it was like a scream of cold up my back and my legs. Bubbles from the impact snaked around my torso and through my hair. When I resurfaced, I gasped in pleasure and shock. The water was about three feet deep, but was enough to wade around in.

I quickly got out again and took off my clothes, taking Teddy out of my pocket and gripping him tightly. I wasn't comfortable losing contact with him for one minute. He was the only thing of home I had left. I slid back in the water, too self-conscious of my body to swim with the other girls.

I stared at the water, turning Teddy over and over again in my palms.

A few minutes later Alice swam over to me. Her hair conveniently covered her breasts as she sat next to me. "That's cute," she said, pointing to Teddy.

"My Dad gave him to me," I said quietly. I was close to tears, and I didn't want to cry while naked, sitting in the middle of a stream. "He's supposed to have some magic in him, but I've never seen it."

"Maybe it doesn't work because you're in a different place," she suggested.

I said nothing.

"You know what magic I love about this place? The spiritual part of it," Alice said, looking up at the sky.

I looked at her with raised eyebrows. "I wouldn't have thought you were the religious type."

"I'm not really," she said loftily, still gazing at the sunrise, "but I like the stories. The Star Goddess is supposedly the daughter of the Sun and the Moon. The constellations are supposed to be signs. If you see the Silver Phoenix, something good will happen to you—things like that."

"Have you seen this Star Goddess?" I asked skeptically.

"I've flown at night and never seen anything," she said. "But it's a nice idea, that at night you have someone looking out for you."

"Is there a dragon constellation?" I asked.

She nodded, smiling. "It symbolizes strength. If you see the Dragon, you'll win a fight, or come out of a hardship triumphant."

"Have you ever prayed to any of the gods?"

"Once," she said. She was quiet so long I thought that was the only thing she was going to say. "The next day I lost my uncle."

A half hour later we got out of the river and went back to camp. Everyone was awake by then, but Zorin had his head in his hands, momentarily letting out a quiet groan. His hair was a mess, and he looked paler than usual.

"What's wrong with him?" I asked Lucide.
He fought back a smile as he said, "He's hung-over."
I laughed, and I saw Bella roll her eyes.
Another day had begun.

Chapter 6: The First Attack

The next day, after Zorin had sobered up, we made our way into the nearest town. When we reached the outside gates, Lucide quickly cleaned up our clothes with his magic glamour. I knew it was only an illusion so we wouldn't look homeless, but it still surprised me what a difference it made. My sneakers, which had been gradually collecting dirt, were now spotless, the shoelaces no longer frayed and splitting. My shirt had collected one or two stains but was now fresh and unwrinkled. I sighed. If only I could have a real shower, I would feel invincible.

We walked into the city, our heads down as we moved among the people going about their daily routines. The cobblestone was filthy, and there was a stench in the air similar to the first city I entered in this world. This time, I thought I could identify the smell: sewage and rotten fish.

I peeked through my bangs and realized not many people were making eye contact either. They kept their heads down and moved quickly, stopping only to swear at people if they bumped into them. Someone passed by and stepped in a puddle, splashing my leg with sledge. I recoiled and bumped into Lucy, hitting the back of my head on her violin case.

"Hey, Blondie!" someone shouted as she steadied me. "I'll give you twenty Doc for whatever's in the box."

I was about to shout something rude back at him, but Lucy put her hand on my shoulder and shook her head.

"Bella," I hissed, still rubbing the sore spot on my head. "What the hell are we doing here?"

"Be quiet, Rose," she said, "I know what I'm doing."

I wanted to say something back, but Lucy put her hand on my arm. Her critical look told me everything she was thinking—I really needed to work more on my temper.

The roads were dirty and the houses were broken. Every house I saw had broken windows; steps leading into a houses were uneven or crumbling, paint was peeling, doors were off their hinges. If Bella thought this was a good place to perform, she was crazy.

Soon we came to the town square. There was a fountain in the middle of the square. When I glanced at the pool of water at its bottom, I noticed there were no coins from people making wishes.

Lucy took out her violin and started playing. Slowly, people began gathering as her song grew longer. Children with bare feet and sucking their thumbs came up timidly and put coins in the empty violin case. Men dug in their pockets to find any stray coins. Women listened with glassy eyes as the song came to an end.

Applause filled the air as women dabbed at their eyes and men put the children on their shoulders.

"Oh, keep going!"

"You have to know more songs!"

"Please keep going!"

Lucy smiled and began a new song; the crowd cheered.

Lucide stood next to Lucy and began forming images with his hands. It was fascinating to watch. His hand would start to move as if he was trying to form something out of clay, and then something would be there, temporarily real, in his hand. He made a few flowers for the women standing in the front row. He handed a small violet to a little girl in a yellow springtime dress, who was eyeing us shyly.

"Do you like the music?" I asked her.

She nodded. I held out my hand. She took it, and I spun her around, her dress spinning out like a little ray of sunshine. She laughed.

When I looked up, I noticed Bella smiling at me approvingly.

Then I noticed a man standing further away than the rest of group. He was leaning against the side of a barbershop, his head bowed, watching us.

I tried to ignore it, but something about him sent chills down my spine. After two or three more songs he still hadn't moved.

I walked around Lucy from behind and came up to Bella.

"We shouldn't be here," I whispered.

"Give it a rest, Rose." Bella said. "We need this."

"It's not that." I jerked my chin in the man's direction. "Does anything about that man seem strange to you? He hasn't moved."

Her eyes widened.

Lucy noticed us whispering and looked at Bella. She mouthed, "wrap it up," before taking my arm and guiding me back to my original place.

"Who is he?" I asked, panic in my voice.

Lucy's song ended. All Bella could do was shake her head.

As the crowd started to move, I glanced over at him. He started walking slowly toward us, and when he saw I was looking at him, he ducked his head and smiled.

"Move with the crowd," Bella said in a calm, level voice. "And I mean move, we're being tailed."

We hustled. My heart had picked up, and my hands were shaking. What did he want? How long had he been following us? What was Bella not telling me?

We started to walk even faster. I could hear the coins clashing against Lucy's violin as she held the instrument close to her chest.

Just as we were about to turn the corner into an alleyway, the man stepped in front of Bella as if he'd stepped out of the wall.

"What are you kids doing here all by yourselves?"

I reeled back and tripped over my feet as Bella screamed and lashed out with her left arm. Ice flew from her fingertips, narrowly missed the man's head, and shattered against a brick wall of the building; then the man was gone.

"Run!" Bella shouted, as she dove into the alley, all of us following.

I didn't have time to think about seeing Bella's power for the first time or what it meant. What would've happened if the man had been hit with the ice? All I could do was run. Lucy was running beside me, and then suddenly she fell back. I stopped to help her up.

She dropped her case and loose coins spilled everywhere across the filthy alley road, making a sound like shattered glass.

The man had Lucy by the hair, his other hand on her throat.

"Hello, everyone," he said, a frightening smile spreading across his face. Everyone had stopped as he suddenly tightened his grip on Lucy's throat.

"You left too quickly. I didn't get to give you anything." He kicked the violin case, which flew across the alley and smashed against the wall, the sound of splintering wood harsh like a whip. I felt a few splinters graze my cheek.

"Let her go," Bella said. Her voice shook.

"Why?" he asked, cocking his head, for a moment, sounding completely sincere.

"Because she's not why you're really here. You want me."

I looked over at her, confused, but she only had eyes for him, watching his hand on Lucy's neck.

"Well, that's not true. You're all a pain in the Drainer's side. He wants you all gone for good." He nodded at Bella. "But he would keep you as a special prize, my dear."

For the first time, Bella looked away.

"I noticed you have a new play thing," the man said, turning his gaze on me. "She's cute. Have you named her yet?"

His hand loosened from Lucy's neck, and he swayed. Lucy took the opportunity to push away from him, and she stumbled. Bella swooped forward and attacked him, knocking him to the ground with a perfectly formed ice ball, rendering him unconscious.

Ginko and I helped Lucy back to her feet. She gripped my hand so tightly I thought I would lose feeling in it.

When I looked up to see what had made the man lose focus, Alice was standing there holding a rock in her right hand.

"Lucy, are you okay?" Alice called to Lucy, dropping the rock.

"We have to keep moving," said Bella, picking up the violin case. "He'll wake up in a minute."

"He's out cold," I said a little too harshly as I gave Lucy my hand. "We have time."

"I say we have about a minute."

"Why do you always counter what I say?" I snapped. "Do you hate me that much?"

Lucy, who had gone pale—from shock or pain, I couldn't really tell—shook her head.

"Wha..."

"I'm saying that because I know I'm right," Bella said. She closed the violin case and handed it back to Lucy, who held it as if it was a new baby. "That thing isn't human, he's a vampire."

I turned as white as a sheet.

We ran.

Out of the alley and out of the town, back deep into the woods. I wanted to stop, but my adrenaline kept me going. There didn't seem to be enough forest in the world to hide us from a vampire. Could he track us somehow? I thought of Jasmine back home, and was for the first time regretting I didn't ask her more questions when I had the chance. Then again, I didn't know how different the vampires of my world were from the ones here.

We ran for another twenty minutes, passing a small place that looked like a ghost town. Finally, when we were all too tired to run anymore, Bella spotted an abandoned house. It appeared to be two stories high. The windows were broken, and the grass around it was so overgrown it almost reached the bottom window. The paint was faded and peeling, and the door was off its hinges, clinging to the frame like a broken tooth.

"We can stay in here for the night," she said as she walked up the steps. "I don't think we should make a fire though. They could find us again too easily." We all followed her into the house.

There was so much dust. It was about three inches thick everywhere it landed. When we first entered the house, there was a broken mirror immediately to my left, above a small ornate table the owner might have placed gloves, or tossed mail onto. It was now missing a leg. The first room to the right was the living room. An ugly brown couch had been upturned, and it was missing a cushion. There was a mirror above the fireplace that had been broken, the glass shining like scattered diamonds on the mantle. Cards for birthdays and anniversaries that had once been on the mantle were all over the floor.

We were all silent. The only sound was the glass from the broken mirrors crunching beneath our feet.

"What happened here?" I finally asked.

No one answered.

As if in a trance, Bella walked very slowly out of the room, making for the front door. I followed close behind. If someone saw us...

But all she did was look again at the broken door. As she was examining it, I noticed an ugly red-brown stain splattered all over it. And at the top, something was engraved.

I froze.

In jagged, spiky writing was that name again. It looked like it had been carved in by a nail:

The Drainer

"Who's the Drainer?" I asked. The vampire had said this disturbing name in the alley, and I wanted answers.

I turned and found everyone had followed behind me. At my question, Lucy's face twisted in an expression of fear. Bella shifted uncomfortably. Alice tucked in her wings. And Zorin looked down at the ground.

"Well—who is he?"

"He's a monster," said Alice. "Bloodthirsty."

"So he's a vampire?"

"No, but close to it," said Bella, finally facing me. "He's a demon."

My head spun. I knew nothing about demons. In my world demons were rarely seen. "What does he do?"

"You know how I draw power from water, right?" Bella asked. "You saw, in the alley?"

I nodded.

"He draws power from an element too." For some reason she seemed reluctant to say.

How bad could that be? I thought. Why does she look so disgusted all of a sudden? What did he draw from? Was it the way he used his powers that had her so repulsed?

"What does he draw from, Bella?"

Her eyes narrowed, her hand tightening on the door handle. I could hear it rattling, just slightly. "Blood," she said finally.

There was a silence I could feel seeping into my bones.

I swallowed hard, feeling sick to my stomach.

"That's why everyone's afraid of him," Zorin continued, taking Bella's hand. "He sends armies out to round people up and take them to his nightmare palace. People that go in never come out: he drains them entirely of blood."

Silence fell again. Bella had a look of pure outrage.

"There's more to it," I said. "That's not the only reason people are afraid of him. They've never seen him before. The only time you see him is when you go to be drained." I shuddered.

"People are more afraid of things they can't see," Bella agreed. " I think he's why you can't go home. You've noticed all the places we visit are half dead, poor, and in ruins. It's because he drains power. The powers people have die when he kills them, so the world is slowly being drained, too. Whenever new power comes in, it's like a flood of water to parched land; he just soaks it up."

"That's why we started a gang," Alice explained. "It's too dangerous to stay in one place. You live your whole life waiting for his armies to knock on your door and drag you off." She shook her head.

"What are his armies made up of?" Was it more demons or just sick-minded humans?

"His army is made up of vampires," said Zorin.

Lucy's face was full of sadness.

"Oh, my God," I said. Then I paused. "Why did the vampire mention you, Bella? He said the Drainer wants you as a prize."

Bella's hair was shading her eyes as she spoke. "He's destroying lives; hundreds of them every day. I escaped the first time they came for me, then started a gang of teenagers that has continued to evade him. He probably wants my head on a spike."

I shook my head, too disturbed to want to believe it. The Drainer.

"One of the worst things is, he lets people know he's come knocking." Alice's voice was warped with hatred. "He writes his name near where he snatches his victims." She pointed at the door, and it wasn't until she did that my slow, fogged brain realized what the stain was: blood.

Chapter 7: The Girl

The man that wasn't a man, the thing known as The Drainer, was restless. His skin was dark blue and covered in warts. His jagged, crooked teeth were stained yellow, and his red eyes looked murderous.

The Drainer paced back and forth in his throne room. The vampire named Ethan stood straight, hands behind his back. Only his eyes moved as he followed the Drainer's movements.

"They have a new member, sir, a young girl with brown hair. She looks to be about sixteen."

"Don't you think I already know that?" the Drainer snapped. "Tell me again," he hissed as he continued pacing, "Why you haven't returned with the girl and her little rag tag of friends?"

"I was ambushed," said the vampire, feeling the back of his head where the blood was drying. "The girl with the wings came up behind me."

"You mean to tell me," the Drainer said in a soft, dangerous voice as he stopped in front of Ethan, "that you were ambushed by that little twit Bella Thompson and her *flying monkey?*"

The flames in the room's fireplace flew into a rage, changing to the color of blood as they leapt out of the hearth, the heat intense and angry.

Ethan seemed to shrink at the physical sight of his master's rage.

A human servant girl named Crissy, with short, curly blonde hair and brown eyes was entering the throne room by the staircase parallel to the fireplace. She'd been carrying a silver tray with a hot towel on it, but dropped the tray in fright when the fire exploded.

The vampire hissed and flew at her, grabbing her throat.

Crissy screamed.

"Enough, Ethan!" the Drainer commanded. There was no sound as he walked up behind him. "There are plenty of villagers for you to snack on. On the other hand..." He reached out, and his long, cold, crooked, blue fingers wrapped around Ethan's neck, choking him instantly. The vampire made a few desperate gagging sounds, his pale fingers grasping at the Drainer's expert chokehold. Then there was a loud, sickening crack, and his body fell to the ground, dead.

Crissy was shaking, her eyes wide with terror and disbelief. Her master, who so often humiliated and tormented her, had just saved her life.

"Stake him through the heart and burn the body," the Drainer ordered. "I have some business to tend to." As he swiftly walked away, leaving the poor servant girl in paralyzed shock, his voice rang out, echoing across the gloomy chamber. "That new girl is the perfect way to bring Thompson to her knees."

Chapter 8: A House Is A Home

The next morning I woke up and didn't know where I was.

It is a really uncomfortable feeling, but, tragically, one I had gotten used to. About two weeks ago, after several failed attempts at world jumping back home, I had to accept that I just wasn't powerful enough yet to make the journey. But now of course I knew the truth: my powers were being drained by a powerful demon—possibly the most powerful demon across all universes.

Every surface in the house was covered in dust. Doors and floorboards creaked; cobwebs were in every corner, often with fat spiders sitting in the middle of them. In some places a vase or a chair was knocked over, and I wondered again what had happened to the people in this house.

Last night I'd found a spare room on the second floor that I shared with Alice. After dusting off the few blankets that had been sitting still for months, we could actually fit in the bed together comfortably enough to sleep through the night. I however, stared out the window across from the bed for hours, wondering if we were going to be found, if the protective spells Bella had put around the property—like she did every night during camp—were going to be enough.

Eventually my nerves did calm down and I was able to sleep. But when I opened my eyes in the morning, there were tears on my cheeks.

I rolled over and Alice wasn't next to me. I sat up, alarm bells ringing, only to have her pop her head around the corner five seconds later.

"Morning, Rose petal," she said, smiling. She ran her hand through her hair, which was still messy from the night's sleep. "You don't mind that I call you that, do you? Of course you don't. We have food in the kitchen if you want some."

"There's food?" I asked, stumbling out of bed. My braid was coming loose, and I could feel the crust of crow's feet at the corner of my eyes.

"Yep!" she nodded. "Might want to wash your face before you go down, though. I'll use the shower after you."

"The shower works?" I'd taken a few baths in rivers since I started traveling with the gang. Hot showers had become a thing of luxury in my mind.

"Yeah. Amazing water pressure too, for such an old dump."

I went into the bathroom with a hairbrush. I turned on the taps, and the nobs creaked in protest from disuse. I managed to get warm water and splashed my face, sighing with pleasure. It had been so long since I'd felt warm water that I could feel my hands shaking while I unbraided my hair.

When I got downstairs, I noticed Bella had already gotten some cleaning done. The floor had clearly been swept, and the kitchen table was clean. On it, was a half eaten loaf of bread and three apples.

"Where did you get the food?" I asked as I sat down.

"Apparently, Alice has been teaching Ginko how to steal," said Bella, smiling. "I can't say I approve, but with no money to buy anything, we really don't have any other options. Go ahead and take an apple and some bread. You, Lucide and I are the only ones who haven't eaten."

"How late is it?" I asked.

"It's only eight, but I guess we're so used to getting up early that nobody else bothered to sleep in."

"Where is Lucide?" I asked, biting into my apple.

"He's out checking on the protective spells," Bella said, smiling as she sat down.

"What?" I asked.

"Nothing."

We both looked up as we heard the door close. "Speak of the devil," Bella said.

"Morning, Bella," Lucide said cheerily as he sat down with us. "I fixed the door as well. It should open normally now." He turned to me. "Morning, Rose petal."

I froze. "Why did you call me that?" I could feel a little bit of heat crawling up my cheeks.

He blushed slightly too, realizing his mistake. "I heard Alice call you that this morning. I hope you don't mind."

"I don't mind at all."

He smiled.

I heard Bella laugh softly, but I was too wrapped up in my own embarrassment to pay any real attention to it.

I forced myself to look away from him and back at Bella. "How long are we staying here?"

"We should be leaving in a few hours," she replied. "After we all take showers."

My heart sank.

"What?" she said, noticing the change in my expression.

"Well," I began, "and don't shoot me, this is just an idea. What if we stayed here, for a while?"

"Rose, it's only a half an hour away from where we were last attacked."

"Exactly! They'd never expect us to settle down. We travel too much. We slept in *beds* last night, Bella! Beds! When is the last time you did that? You've been at this longer than I have."

She looked down at her hands. "It has been a while."

"We'd be hiding in plain sight, especially with the disguises Lucide can do. Why would they think to come looking for us here?"

"Well..." she trailed off, then looked at Lucide. "What do you think?"

"Rose does have a point," he said, and my heartbeat picked up. From excitement or the flattery, I couldn't tell. "Think about it. The only times we've ever been attacked is when we're traveling, when the protective spells are down. If we stayed here, there'd be no need to take them down, so we'd be invisible to his people. No one would come looking in here, the door is already marked, and the place is already cursed."

I shuddered.

"We could also put up illusions spells, to keep the place looking corroded so no one would think something was up. When we went into town we could wear disguises. This place could be home."

"What about earning money? If we perform in the same

place, people could start talking."

"So whenever we need money we travel a bit, then come back. It wouldn't be that bad."

She sat back. "I can't argue with that." She thought about it for a moment. "Let's do it. I'll go tell the others."

You're not going to ask them what they think?" I asked.

She looked at me and smiled. The smile, for the first time in a while, seemed completely warm and genuine. "Are you honestly suggesting they would mind?"

So that was that. The house became home that quickly. We set about cleaning, using magic spells to make the process go faster. Dust was everywhere, and there were cobwebs, broken glass, and dead mice stuffed away in corners. Bella and Lucide were constantly checking the protective spells every few hours, especially the illusion spells, that from the outside would make the house appear run down, and the spells that made *us* invisible when we passed a window or went out on the lawn.

I swept, dusted, scrubbed, and polished everything that wasn't being cleaned by magic. I didn't want Bella regretting for even a second she'd asked me to stay here. Alice and I straightened up our room, and she began talking excitedly about eventually painting the walls, and perhaps buying a second bed. I was too embarrassed to ask, but I wondered when she'd last spent even a few days in a home.

When evening approached and the sun began to set, I opened a window and watched the sun go down, feeling almost as if I were back home at last.

The next morning, the first thing I did was open all of the windows. It was springtime, and the sun was shining by eight in the morning. We ate what was left of the bread, Bella reminding us we'd have to perform soon to earn more money. Cheerful for the first time in days, I went out in the yard to look for flowers to put in a vase.

In the back yard, I found a small patch of daisies planted beside an apple tree. I knelt down to admire them and pick some, when I heard footsteps behind me.

I whirled around.

It was Lucide.

"Whoa, there," he said, putting his hands up in mock surrender. "It was your idea to stay here. Don't tell me now you're getting jumpy."

"I'm sorry," I said. "Habit."

"I see you found some daisies."

"I thought they'd make the house smell nice."

"And it would be a nice touch of color."

"That too, I guess."

He picked one and held it out to me. As I reached for it, it transformed into a red rose.

"I like roses better," he said.

I held it delicately in my hand. "You've got to teach me how to do that."

He laughed. "I don't know if you're able to learn magic from this world," he said not unkindly. "With your own powers not working, you might not be able to develop..." He trailed off, at loss for how to phrase the dark reality.

I laid down on the grass, looking up at the clear blue sky. I didn't want to tell him I was scared out of my wits. How little I had thought of my family after coming here. I closed my eyes. I couldn't afford to have attachments; I was going home the first chance I got.

I felt him lie down next to me, and I felt him gently take my hand, intertwining his fingers with mine.

Maybe just this once.

Chapter 9: We Are Targets

Over the next three days, we managed to bring in a little more money without having to travel. Wearing a disguise, Bella went to town and sold the table with a missing leg for twenty Doc. She'd substituted the missing leg with one of Lucide's illusion charms.

Living in the house made me feel as if I had a family again. On the fourth day, Ginko used his light powers to put small balls of lights on the ceiling once the sun went down. They looked like small orbs, making me sorry I'd ever called him a firefly. Plus, the lights gave the perfect excuse for a dance party. Lucy played her violin, and we skipped around the living room, trading dance partners and laughing. I danced with Lucide, Ginko, and even Alice as the room and lights spun like some crazy carnival ride.

I couldn't remember the last time I'd had so much fun. I danced until I was dizzy and laughed until my stomach ached. The protective spells held, and I felt safe for the first time in weeks.

Alice took me out on the porch and showed me the stars. To my surprise, they weren't silver anymore, but all the colors of the rainbow. Red, purple, blue and yellow stars sparkled in the sky.

"This happens on every full moon," Alice explained, as I looked up in awe. "The Star Goddess is blessing the night."

"I still don't know if I believe in a woman that lives in the stars," I said. "But it's beautiful."

"It's great for romance, too," she said. When I looked at her sharply, she wiggled her eyebrows and laughed.

Back inside, Lucy was still playing her violin. Lucide was over at the fireplace, making the flames dance in time with the music. Ginko was sitting on the couch and smiling, but not dancing with anyone.

I took my braid and pinned it up at the back of my head, then I marched over to him. Lucy had just started playing a new song.

"Can I have this dance?" I asked. When he looked up at me in surprise, I smiled. "I can draw a mustache on myself if you want."

He took my hand, and I spun him.

Lucy's song picked up pace. It was a lively, happy tune, something that seemed so welcoming after so many days in the woods. I felt Ginko laugh as we spun and skipped around. He looked like he was having fun, completely stress free for the first time since I'd met him. I felt a rush of affection toward him, happy to see him happy.

The song ended and we all clapped as Lucy put her violin down and rubbed her sore hands, collapsing on the couch. Within no time, she was asleep.

Eventually I fell asleep on the couch as well, too tired to climb the stairs to my room.

On the sixth day is when everything turned into a nightmare.

We were eating breakfast when Bella got up to get a drink of water. When she turned the tap, no water came out. She pulled her hands back, twisting them coaxingly, trying to tempt the water out with her power, but nothing happened. She did it again and again with no result.

"What's wrong with it?" she asked. She hid it well, but I could hear the undertone of panic in her voice.

"Calm down," Zorin said. "This is an old house, it might just be the pipes."

Bella and Lucide locked eyes. "It could be that, or..."

"Or he knows we're here," Lucide finished.

"Don't be ridiculous," I said. "How is that possible? And why would he turn off the water?"

"His main target is me," Bella reminded me. "And the only way I can use my powers is by using water. He could be trying to starve us out."

"Don't be silly," Ginko said. "There are more ways to get water than kitchen faucets."

"Exactly. If we have to leave the house to get it, we leave the protective charms behind. That's when he gets us."

"Then you don't leave the house," I said.

"What?" she asked.

I stood up. I felt weird taking charge, but someone had to do it. "I'll take the rest of the money, go to town, and get some food and water. It'll be alright."

For the first time, she looked at me with respect in her eyes. "There's only eight Nil left."

"Doesn't matter," I said, shaking off my nerves.

"Alright," Bella said briskly. "Get your disguise ready. Lucide and Lucy, go with her."

I went upstairs two at a time, a nervous knot forming in my stomach.

Twenty minute later, we left the house, our eye color and hair changed completely. I had black hair that reached down to my shoulders and wide, sky-blue eyes. Lucy had short, curly red hair and eyes that matched mine. Lucide had short, wavy brown hair and dark gray eyes. The charms would last for only a half an hour.

We walked quickly, trying to act natural, our hearts jumping with anxiety. We all knew that if there were vampires hunting us in this area, visual disguises might not be enough. We still had a scent that was hard to get rid of.

I looked around and for the first time, really noticed the behavior of the people. Everyone was timid, skittish. Children stuck close to their parents, eye contact was quickly dropped. Before we left that morning, I'd spent some time looking out the window, people watching. I'd tried to see what I was about to step out into. I'd seen people walking fast, as if everyone knew exactly where they were going, and didn't want to be interrupted.

I was in the lead, clutching my basket, trying my hardest to focus on the task at hand. We were just going to get food. That was all.

Someone bumped into me and I dropped the basket. I bent over to pick it up.

"Rose," said Lucide slowly, quietly.

I closed my eyes.

"Rose, turn around and come over here, please."

I opened my eyes and very slowly turned back around.

A vampire was towering over me. He was grinning; two sharp, pointed fangs glistening with saliva. I suddenly felt small, looking up into his hungry face.

No. No. No. No. No. No. No.

"Shit."

The vampire came down on me, and at the last second I rolled to the ground, kicking him in the jaw. I could feel the ache in my bone where my foot had collided with his face and I felt the powerful beginnings of a head rush coming on, but adrenaline pushed it all out. "Get away from me!" I screamed.

My shout seemed to startle the crowd, and the street turned into a river of high-pitched noise as people screamed and ran for cover.

Fear and anger were mixing together, making me dizzy. As the thing ran at me again I swung a punch, using all my energy. It managed to dodge my swing, and in the same split second, grabbed me from behind.

"Hello, sweetheart," it hissed in my ear.

I yelped out of fear and pain as its hand tightened on my neck—to break it, or choke me I couldn't tell—and then it screamed.

In a fit of adrenaline-filled rage, Lucide had rushed forward with his palms out, already glowing with orange fire and planted his palms on the vampire's face. It screamed and let go of me, and Lucy rushed forward to help me up.

The vampire punched Lucide, and he fell with a cry. Then it turned and kicked my foot. I heard a loud crack and screamed as pain exploded.

Lucy put her arms around me protectively as the vampire slowly kneeled to my level.

"Well, that was fun," he said, his voice a soft purr. "I like this little game we're playing. I'll see you later, Rosie."

And then, faster than I could blink, he disappeared. Lucide sat up.

"You just bitch slapped a vampire," I said, dumbfounded, as he helped me to my feet.

"Yeah, well, let's get you back to the house. We need to do

something about that ankle."

"Don't freak out," I said as Lucy and Lucide eased me back through the front door.

"Don't freak out?" asked Bella in an indignant voice. "You broke your ankle!"

I cried out as pain pierced my leg.

"We'll get you to a doctor," Bella promised, but her promise was thin.

I laughed, the sound harsh because of the pain.

"Why is that so funny?" Bella snapped.

"Because we can't afford a doctor, let alone the medication."

She had nothing to say to that.

"I'll take you to the doctor," said Zorin after the silence had lengthened. "We'll steal the medication if we have to. How well can you walk?"

"Not well," I admitted breathlessly.

He picked me up gracefully. His muscles were so firm it was like lying on stone. I blushed just slightly.

"Take this," said Lucide, tossing Zorin the practically empty bag of money. His eyes were hard.

"Thanks," I whispered in Zorin's ear as he carried me out the door. I could feel Bella's worried eyes boring into my back.

"Once part of the Rags and Riches gang, always part of the gang. You're family, Rose. I don't mind at all."

"What about when we get there and they ask for our names?"

"We'll deal with it." His voice had gone as hard as Lucide's eyes.

"You know, I think Lucide is jealous of you," I said to keep him talking.

"Why wouldn't he be?" He was grinning. "I'm carrying a beautiful woman away in my arms."

I would have punched him if he hadn't been carrying me. I blushed. "Lucide would never say something like that if it were Bella."

"Just not out loud," he amended.

"Oh, shut up."

Zorin chuckled, but didn't say anything else.

A few minutes later we reached the village. "It feels weird being this close to civilization," Zorin muttered.

"It is a little unsettling," I agreed. He held me closer.

"May I help you?" asked a voice behind us.

I started. "Damn," Zorin said, then turned. "I'm looking for the closest doctor."

"Another half mile straight ahead," said the stranger. "Do you need help getting there?" he asked, with a concerned look at me.

"No, I can manage, thank you."

The stranger shrugged, shook off his concern and walked away.

"That was close," I hissed.

"At least we know where the doctor is," Zorin said tightly.

We finished the journey in silence.

We arrived at a small brick house with vines climbing the frame. There were windows covered with white lace curtains and a sign on the door that said, "Sick and Injured, Always Welcome."

Zorin and I exchanged glances. "It says always welcome," I said timidly.

Zorin kicked the door open.

A woman was sitting across from us with her back to us at a desk. When she heard the door open, she turned with start. Then seeing me being held by Zorin, her face softened with motherly concern.

"Broken ankle, dear?" Her tone said she'd seen this a hundred times. She had sympathetic blue eyes and blonde hair pulled back in a bun. She couldn't be older than thirty.

"Yes," I said. Now that our journey was over, I began to really feel the pain.

"Lie her down on the bed here," she said to Zorin. I groaned, half with pain, half with exhaustion. Zorin sat down next to me on the bed, staying far enough away from my ankle to make sure he wasn't hurting me. Regardless of his efforts, I could feel sweat beading on my brow. My body wasn't taking this very well.

"It's okay, Rose; you're safe."

"Nowhere is safe," I hissed back.

"Of course you're safe here, dear," said the doctor, coming back with ice. "You're from the Rags and Riches gang, aren't you?"

"What?" my voice rose an octave. Zorin's eyes had gone wide. His hand froze as he was reaching for mine to calm me.

"Relax, dear, I'm not going to turn you in," said the nurse soothingly. "I go to your street concerts whenever I can. I think it's despicable what the Drainer is trying to do to you."

I relaxed, but not completely. I could see Zorin's shoulders were still tense.

"Before I put the cast on to set the break, can I have your name for the record?"

"The record?" I asked nervously.

"Just for medical purposes."

"Oh right. Of course," I said, feeling lightheaded. "Before I do any of that, can I use your bathroom?"

"Of course. Can I help you get there?"

"No, Zach can," I said hurriedly.

Zorin picked me up and brought me to the bathroom.

"A record? We're screwed!" I said, once he set me down on the toilet seat.

"Calm down," said Zorin.

"How can I calm down? The Drainer will be able to track us again!"

"We'll give fake names. Apparently my name is Zach."

"Do you think that will be enough?"

"It has to be."

I sighed, biting my lip. My good leg bounced up and down in anxiety. "Okay, let's go back out."

"Have you thought of a name?"

"Yeah."

He nodded, put his arm around my waist, and supported me out of the bathroom back into the doctor's office.

"Everything okay?" asked the doctor when we got back.

"Yes, thank you."

"So then, what's that name?"

"Emily Jameson."

She scribbled it on her board. "Let's get that ankle fixed."

Once she fixed my leg and gave me medication to numb the pain, I felt a lot better. The cast was firm and supporting. I felt bad that we were planning to steal medicine from her, but I reminded myself that if we could pay, we would. And in a few days time, Bella would probably be able to heal it completely. On the way to the doctors, Zorin told me how Bella had the power to heal wounds; but if she wasn't hydrated, she wouldn't be able to heal so much as a paper cut.

"I'll go get your prescription," the doctor said, and went to the back room.

"Can we pay her?" I whispered.

Zorin took the coin purse out of his pocket and counted what was left. He shook his head.

My heart sank.

The doctor came back in. "Here you go, Emily," she said. "Take two pills a day, about five hours apart. That should take care of the pain and help you heal in a week or two."

"Thank you," I said, and took the medicine.

"I'll walk you out," she said, and headed toward the door.

I looked at Zorin in confusion. He looked as confused as I did, shrugged, and helped me walk out.

When we got to the door, about twenty grinning vampires were blocking our way.

In the silence, my voice rang out. "Shit."

"I'm sorry, dear," said the doctor. The vampires pushed her back, and she disappeared into the mob.

I tried to turn, but I found myself pinned against the building's brick wall. A vampire had his hand on my throat, his crooked grin in my face. My casted foot hung limply, and I heard Zorin cry out in pain.

"Zorin!" I shouted.

"He can't help you," said the vampire holding me. "You stupid girl."

I struggled, gagging slightly as his grip on my throat tightened.

"We're not here to hurt you. We just wanted to get you

back on our grid. Our friend at the market can't have all the fun. Where's your boyfriend?"

"Go to hell," I rasped.

He grinned. Before I could blink, he punched me. I cried out and fell to the ground, gripping that side of my face. It felt as if my face had been slammed into a cement wall. When I opened my eyes, the vampires and the doctor were gone.

"Zorin?" I heard him groan, and then I found him, lying on his back. "Zorin!"

"I'm okay," he said, and sat up. "Why didn't they take us?"

"I don't know. That stupid bitch!" I shouted, and threw the medicine. The pills spilled out onto the road, and I couldn't care less.

"Why'd you do that?" Zorin demanded.

"I can handle pain," I said bitterly. "Besides, since she was working for them, they might have been poisoned."

He stumbled to his feet and helped me up. "Come on."

When we stumbled back into the house a half hour later, the gang was eagerly awaiting our arrival. Bella tried to smile when she saw me in the cast, but her smile faltered when she saw the look on Zorin's face.

"What happened?"

"The Drainer happened," I growled, as Zorin lowered me into a chair.

"What did he do?" Bella urgently asked Zorin, who tried to calm her.

I turned and found myself engulfed in Lucide's arms. I hugged him back, surprised by this sudden affection.

"Are you okay?" he asked.

"I'm fine. I didn't get the medicine."

"I should have gone with you."

"Don't be stupid," I said. "There was nothing you could have done. They just wanted us back on their grid, that's all."

He hugged me tighter, and I allowed a single tear to leak out of my eye.

Chapter 10: Curiosity Killed the Kat

We left just an hour later. To my extreme embarrassment, Zorin and Lucide took turns carrying me, and Bella promised she would heal me as soon as she could find water. I didn't really care anymore; I didn't have any energy. All I wanted to do was cry and sleep. Sometimes I did both, waking up in either Zorin's or Lucide's arms with tears staining my cheeks.

After about two hours, the sun began to set, and because we were desperate to rest, Lucide cast disguises on us all and knocked on someone's door. At best they'd invite us inside; at worst, they'd direct us to the nearest inn.

We must've really been a sight. I tried to imagine what we all looked like: our clothes were torn and mud-splattered; we were half starved. Even Lucide's spell couldn't hide that. I fully expected the person opening the door to shriek and slam it shut.

But the person who opened the door was a teenager, maybe a year older than me. What startled me, however, was this girl's appearance—she was a cat. She had a fur-covered face strikingly resembling a cat's features—brown and white fur, a pointed nose tipped with pink and ice-blue eyes. On top of a river of perfect golden hair, two brown cat ears peeked out, attentive and listening.

As I stared at her, Alice leaned over to me. "Not what you were expecting, is she?" She laughed under her breath so that the cat-girl couldn't hear.

But apparently she had, for her ears went flat against her hair although the expression in her eyes didn't change. "Who are you?" she snapped.

"Please," Bella said in her most persuasive voice. "We need shelter, if only for the night. Our friend is hurt," she gestured toward me, cradled in Zorin's arms.

The girl looked at me, probably trying to gauge whether or not I was actually hurt.

"My ankle is broken," I said. "We can't afford a doctor. But Bella is a healer. If you give her some water I'll be better in a few minutes."

The girl evaluated me for a few more seconds before she nodded and ushered us into the little room behind her, giving Alice a quick glare as she passed.

The house's first floor was a wide-open space, the front door leading into the kitchen. There was a kitchen table with humorously mismatching dining chairs clustered around it. To the right was a living room with a couch and coffee table, a strange, spiky houseplant placed in the center of it. At the back of the room was a set of stairs leading up to the second floor.

"What happened to you?" the cat-girl asked as she gestured for me to sit down on a kitchen chair.

"Ambushed by the Drainer's army." Bella saved me from answering as she rolled up her sleeves to work on my ankle. Her voice carried so much exhaustion in it that Zorin put an arm around her.

"You can stay here," said the cat-girl at once, almost too quickly. She filled a glass of water, and handed it to Bella, who finished it in three gulps. She put both of her hands on my ankle. I took a deep breath as I felt a stab of pain.

"My name is Kat," said the girl. "What are your names?"

I paused, wondering if Bella or Lucide would give out aliases. Lucide did, lying with ease, but I was in too much pain to remember my name. Hopefully we wouldn't be here long enough for it to matter.

"I'll put on something hot," Kat said when we were done with the fake introductions. "Do you have any preferences? Tea or hot chocolate? "

"Tea for all of us would be fine," Bella said, cutting off Ginko's vote for hot chocolate. He started grumbling and she gave him a look.

"Tea it is, then," Kat agreed. She turned to the little stove, revealing to us her brown cat's tail.

Alice snickered.

Kat's ears flattened, and she let out a low hiss.

"Knock it off, Alice," Bella whispered.

Bella then let go of my ankle. "Just don't run any marathons," she teased as I stood up with Lucide's help.

Kat had two adjoining rooms that we shared. Zorin, Bella, Alice, and I were in one room; Lucide, Ginko, and Lucy were in the other. A door connected the two rooms, which I appreciated. It felt strange sleeping in someone else's house not knowing how the others were doing.

After drinking the tea and thanking Kat again for her hospitality, we went up to our rooms, leaving the connecting door open a crack. There was a window across from the bed I was sharing with Alice, the curtain only half closed. I watched the moon peek at me as it rose higher in the sky.

About fifteen minutes after being in bed, I heard the other bed shift. Keeping my eyes closed, I listened. I heard someone sit up.

"Bella?" someone whispered. Zorin.

"I can't sleep," Bella whispered back.

"It's only been fifteen minutes." I heard him get up and walk across the room and sit next to her. "What's wrong?"

"Paranoia, I guess. I just can't shake the feeling that something's wrong."

"You're not paranoid," said Zorin. "You're just trying to protect the gang. You've been a good leader. Stop worrying and get some sleep."

"Am I?"

"Are you what?"

"A good leader. Sometimes I think Alice would be a better leader."

"I'd be a little worried about your sanity if you chose her."

"The way I acted when you were drunk. Lucide—even *Rose* was a better leader. While I ran around freaking out, Lucide gave orders while Rose calmed me down."

"No one is expecting you to be Wonder Woman, Bellie. You do the best you can. That's why you have Lucide as backup."

I heard their weight shift; Bella was probably taking his hand.

"I love you. Do you know that?" The fondness in her voice was hard to miss.

"That's why I'm here." I heard them kiss and then Zorin said, "Get some sleep," and he went back to bed.

After sleeping all night, I was the best rested I'd been in weeks. I stretched and groaned happily as the others began to stir. Alice was already sitting up and by the hard look in her eyes; I could tell she'd also overheard Bella and Zorin's secret talk last night.

Bella swung her legs onto the floor. I think she was the happiest of all of us to be awake. She liked when we were moving and in action. She didn't like staying in one place too long.

Once everyone was up we trooped down to the kitchen. Kat was not yet up, so the kitchen was cold and silent.

"I'll make some tea," Bella said, padding across the floor in her socks. One of the socks had a hole revealing her big toe.

"Cocoa!" Ginko protested. I saw Lucide shake his head at him.

"Fine, cocoa, then," Bella agreed. Ginko stared at her like she was an alien and Zorin smiled. I guess the full night's sleep was putting her in good spirits.

The smell of hot chocolate woke Kat up. Her ears pricked as she smelled the air appreciatively. "Smells good!"

"I hope you don't mind," Bella said sheepishly.

"Why would I mind hot chocolate?" Kat smiled at her kindly. "Anyway, why don't you guys take showers and I can make breakfast."

We all paused, unsure about the sudden offer.

"Why don't you go first?" Kat suggested to Bella, and Bella's eyes narrowed. Only when she got nods from both Lucide and Zorin did she leave for the bathroom.

Kat took Bella's place and began putting ingredients in a bowl. "Pancakes," she muttered. "Lily, can you get me two eggs?"

I did as she asked.

Lucide cleared his throat. "It's very nice of you to feed us."

"Hmm..." she said, distracted, as she put flour into the bowl. "You're second in command, aren't you?"

"Um, yeah, I guess I am." He and Zorin exchanged glances. Alice moved to stand by my side.

In the sudden silence we could hear Bella's shower starting.

Kat's ears had gone flat.

"I'm sorry."

Before any of us could react the door burst open and vampires came pouring through.

"Put your hands in the air!" one shouted.

Alice's wings transformed and flapped out, knocking me slightly to the side. When one vampire dove for us, I raised my hands.

"Stop it!"

I tried to lift up a chair and throw it at the vampire, but faster than I could see, the vampire had my hands behind my back. Before I knew it, he had bitten me and I let out an agonized scream.

An infuriated look lighting his eyes, Lucide lunged at the vampire, but was knocked aside with one quick swipe from the vampire's arm.

In no time at all, the vampires managed to round us up in a packed circle, herding us to the center of the room.

Upstairs a door burst open—Bella, realizing what was happening. She came running down the stairs, hair dripping, towel wrapped around her. "*Shit!* Kat, you beast!"

A vampire flew at her and had her before she could raise a hand. "Shut up," it hissed.

"No," Bella sobbed.

"Oh, yes, darling," the vampire purred. "This is your invitation to the Drainer's Dinner Party."

Bella whimpered.

"Bella, I'm so sorry," Kat said.

"Shut up, you bitch!" Bella shrieked.

"Oh no, no, no, don't say that," said the vampire holding her. "Because she's coming with you."

Kat's eyes widened. "You said if I gave you the Rags and Riches Gang, you'd let me go!"

"What's a little white lie?" hissed the vampire. He tugged

on Bella's hair, and she gasped in pain. "I'm going to take this one to get changed, and then we'll be on our way." He began to jerk Bella up the stairs.

We were all pulled out the door.

Our hands were bound with cuffs around our wrists. We each had about four feet of chain connecting our wrists. The chains for our ankles were less forgiving, about two feet from ankle to ankle. Surprisingly, they didn't check our pockets, and Teddy was still safely tucked away in mine.

Five minutes after Bella was dragged up the stairs by her hair, she came out of the house, escorted by the vampire. She was dressed, with her hair still drying. As she closed the front door behind her, I noticed ice was forming on the handle. Looking around, I saw the windows icing over, and from the ground up, ice was covering the house, crawling over it like a virus as it slowly covered the outside of the house completely.

Bella gave Kat a death glare before she allowed herself to be chained up, her head held high.

We could still walk, but it was hard. It was easy to trip on the ankle chains, then be roughly pulled to my feet by my hair. I was walking next to Lucide and could see he was badly beaten. He had a purple eye and a split lip that was clotting with dried blood.

"Hey," I whispered. "Thanks for trying to rescue me."

He snorted. "Some good it did us." He lowered his voice even more. "I think the chains somehow disable our powers. I've tried to burn my bonds away, but nothing's happened."

"Keep moving!" growled a vampire.

I nodded and fell silent, deep in thought.

The sun climbed, and we marched on. The hotter it got, the more I felt like the sun was a demon eye staring down at us, laughing. We had failed, and the Drainer had us at last. After years of cat and mouse, the last swipe of the cat's paw captured the elusive teenaged gang.

I was marching next to Bella. She looked more pale and tired than terrified.

"Are you okay?" I whispered.

She tried to smile. "I tried leading and failed."

"You didn't fail us."

"I should have never let us go in that house."

"You had no way of knowing Kat would betray us."

She looked a thousand years old when she spoke next. "There's something I need to tell you. I haven't told anyone except Zorin."

"What is it?"

She pulled up her sleeve to expose the skin up to her shoulder. I had to peer very hard to see what was there, and then I almost threw up.

Etched—scarred—into the middle part of Bella's upper arm were two words: The Drainer. The scar was whiter than the paleness of her arm, permanently part of her skin.

"Oh my God!" I said breathlessly.

Bella took down her sleeve again to hide her secret. "I'm his daughter."

Part 3

Chapter 11: The Drainer

We were dragged to him in the chains.

We reached the palace sooner than I'd expected. It looked like something out of nightmares: all the plants and vegetation in the surrounding grounds were dead or decaying. There was a rotting, putrid smell that reminded me of corpses.

The castle itself was terrifying. Built with black stone, it looked like it was crumbling, with vines creeping up to block the tall, narrow windows. The window frames were dark and splintering, the glass panes so thin they looked like they would shatter at next winter's frost. The stone walls were black and slick—the doors we were dragged through were at least thirty feet tall.

Even though my ankle was healed, I felt my feet dragging as we were pulled to the middle of his throne room.

He was smiling. When he saw Bella, she wouldn't look at him. He walked over to her and put three fingers under her chin. I heard her gasp in pain.

"Hello, sweetheart," he purred.

She glared back at him.

He kept looking at her, never blinking, as if he'd gotten hold of some unattainable prize. His fingers moved from under her chin to cupping her face, and I heard her cry out. I couldn't imagine having him as a father. The pain he had caused her over the years must have been monumental.

I wondered if anyone had heard her tell me her secret. I glanced at the spot on her arm where the scar was, but the Drainer wasn't concerned with it.

He leaned down and kissed her on the forehead. She gasped, holding back another strangled cry of pain.

"Send them to the dungeons," he commanded to the vampires behind us. "I'll deal with them later."

The dungeon was dark and damp. The vampires had taken our shoes, and the floor was freezing. Lucide must've been right about the chains being able to drain our powers, because I was feeling exhausted from more than just the walk to the palace.

We were all quiet, listening to the place around us. Occasionally I saw a rat run from shadow to shadow. Water dripped down from the walls. There were no windows. The floor we were sitting on was covered in green-brown grime. Our chains were connected to the wall, still attached to our wrists, so each of us had about five feet of chain to move our arms. A few times I tried tugging at them, pulling at the chains fruitlessly. The sound as they rattled and banged against the wall made my head hurt.

I was chained next to Bella, and she didn't speak. Traces of tears were left on her face, but I couldn't remember seeing her cry. I wondered what was going through her head, being back in the palace that she must have grown up in. Had she ever spent time in the dungeons? What had the Drainer done to her? But I didn't dare ask.

Ginko was chained next to Kat, and he was the first to ask her. "Why did you do it? Why did you turn us in?"

Kat took a deep breath before answering. "A few days ago, the Drainer's army came for me. As I plead for my life, I told him I'd turn the Rags and Riches Gang in if I saw you. There had been rumors floating around that you'd been spotted in my village. For some reason he believed me, and he let me go."

"He must've known we'd settled down at that point," Zorin said, his hands in fists.

"I was just blabbing, I didn't know what I was saying..."

"Like hell you didn't," I snarled.

"Rose," Lucide cautioned. "We're here now. It can't be helped."

I didn't know what to say after that.

After about twenty minutes of silence, Bella spoke. She didn't lift her head, and her hair was hiding her eyes.

"You never said anything." She addressed this to no one, which made us look at each other, puzzled.

"What?" I asked.

"Lucide. You never said anything." She looked up then, and her eyes were rimmed with red. "Whenever someone asked about the Drainer, I lied and said I didn't know why he wanted me. You must've seen through it, yet you never said anything." She never broke eye contact with him, brown looking into blue, never blinking.

"I figured if it was something you wanted us to know, you'd tell us." His tone was sincere, and he looked at her with admiration in his eyes. "I trust you, Bella."

That's when we heard the door open. We all tensed. It didn't sound like someone coming down the stairs with purpose, a vampire to come drag us away. The steps were light, even hesitant.

It was a maid, carrying a tray with a loaf of bread and a jug of what I hoped was water. She was wearing a long gray ankle-length dress, and an apron, covered in dirt, ash and grease. She had short, curly blonde hair and brown eyes. The look in her eyes were sad, as if she knew us, and didn't want to see us sentenced to death.

"Crissy?" Bella said, her voice surprised and indignant at the same time.

"Erika!" Crissy shrieked.

Erika?

"What are... what..." Her eyes filled with tears. "Oh, Erika, he can't."

"I'm afraid he already has," she said through gritted teeth.

"But...is there anything I can do?"

"Not unless you have the key to our chains."

She shook her head sadly. "He keeps it around his neck at all times."

Bella turned toward us. "Everyone, this is Crissy. She's a maid of the Drainer's who has helped me through some really hard times."

To my surprise, she bobbed a curtsy in our general direction. "It's nice to meet you all. I'm sorry it's under tragic circumstances." She knelt to the ground and began slicing the bread, passing one piece out to each of us. Then she poured a glass of water for each of us, passing that out. Giving Bella a cup, she paused. "Erika, perhaps I could talk to him."

"No. That's a death sentence, Crissy."

"Serving him is a death sentence."

"You've survived this long, haven't you?"

"He saved my life the other day."

Bella froze. "What happened?"

"A vampire that had been sent to capture you came back empty handed. He—the vampire—flew at me in his rage and tried..." Her voice trembled on the last word. "The Drainer stopped him. He killed him."

"I still don't want you talking to him, Crissy. He will kill you."

"I would die for you."

Tears poured down Bella's face as she looked at her old friend. "I love you, Crissy. That's why you can't do this. You're my sister in every way." Bella's chains rattled as she leaned forward and hugged the terrified maid. "If you remember anything about me, remember that."

Crissy hugged her back, then pulled away. "I must go. They're expecting me in the kitchen."

"Crissy!" Bella called after her as she fled up the stairs. "Promise me!"

"I promise. I love you, Erika."

After that, it was only the waiting.

Kat sat in her own corner, hugging her knees, her ears flat against her hair. A small cut on her cheek was still leaking blood. Nobody paid her any attention. She was the traitor, the reason we were in this nightmare.

It began to get colder as we sat in our own little corners of hell, waiting for the devil to rattle our chains.

If only to distract myself from the blocks of ice that were now my feet, I asked Bella, "Why did Crissy call you Erika?"

It took her a few seconds to reply. "That's my real name. I didn't want to use it because the Drainer named me; at least that's what he always said. I never wanted to have anything to do with him. Isabella was my mom's name."

"What happened to her?" I asked.

"He killed her after I was born." She took a deep breath. "I never even knew what she looked like."

"Bella, I'm so sorry."

"Thanks," she said, looking down at the floor. "At least you know the truth now. And Rose?"

"Yeah?"

"I'm sorry we couldn't get you back home."

I reached out and took her hand, gripping it tight. Her fingers were as cold as ice. "It's alright. I'm with family here, too."

She smiled and put her arm around me.

Roughly a half an hour later we heard the door open again. For a space of two seconds my spirits soared, thinking it was Crissy, coming back and saying she had somehow convinced the Drainer to spare our lives.

The fantasy was shattered like broken glass when a vampire rounded the corner. We all shrank as he grinned at us. He was tall and pale, like they all seemed to be. Short, messy, brown hair topped his head, and his eyes were black. They glittered in the darkness and drank us in, as if vampires fed on souls, not blood.

"Well, now," he purred. "Who wants the first invitation upstairs?"

Alice whimpered. No one spoke.

The vampire looked at us in turn, each of us avoiding his gaze. After a few moments, during which I didn't breathe, his gaze settled on Lucide. He walked toward him casually, his moves relaxed and lazy. Lucide tensed up.

I cried out as Lucide swung at him, but the vampire laughed as he dodged the blow, taking out a key to unlock Lucide's chains. Not at the wrist, but at the wall. They must have wanted to keep them on, so the victims didn't gain their powers back in time to have a chance at challenging the Drainer.

This couldn't be happening. I never imagined they would drag us away one by one. Somehow I didn't think the Drainer would be capable of psychological torture—he was too power hungry.

Everyone was shouting now, profanities and empty threats poured out of our mouths like water. Chains rattled and clanked as we pulled at the wall, more desperate than ever to break free and fight. The vampire, laughing at our pathetic efforts, kept Lucide at bay and grabbed him by the back of the neck.

"Fight anymore and I'll break your neck. It'll only make death that much more painful for you."

It was then that Lucide finally went limp, defeated and weak. The vampire held him firmly under the elbow and dragged him toward the exit. I could feel tears on my cheeks, and right before he rounded the corner, I whimpered his name.

He looked back at me, his blue eyes large and sad. Then he looked away, and was gone.

When I heard the door close, I couldn't speak. I sat back against the wall, the cold and roughness of it against my back; I could smell the mildew that had grown long ago.

I didn't know my head was in Bella's lap until I found myself crying again, clutching her shirt like a small child. She pet my hair and murmured softly, but I never heard the words. Half frozen, I fell asleep in her arms to the sound of my own weeping.

And they did that to each of us, a different vampire coming each time, as if they all wanted to glory in our pain. Lucy was next, then Alice, Ginko, Zorin, and Kat. Nothing stopped us from trying to break from our chains every time one of us were torn away, screaming threats and curses that could never come to light. The worst part was the screams. When we were all quiet, the only sound other than the scurrying of rat feet, was the loan, painful scream. It was muffled by walls, but still there.

When they came for Kat, she backed up against the wall, her eyes wide. "Bella, I'm sorry! I'm so sorry! No stop it," she sobbed as she was dragged away, punching and struggling whenever she could. "Bella, please! I'm sorry! No! No!"

"Kat!" Bella shouted as she was dragged out of our sight. "Kat!" But just like all the others, she was gone with the slam of the heavy door, and we were alone again.

It was just Bella and I, sitting alone in the dark, quiet cold that was the first threshold of death. We sat holding hands, and I swore I could feel her heart beating through her fingertips. Tears were frozen on my face.

"You know, I dreamed of this one day being all over," she said, her black hair matted, wet with her tears. "I dreamed that one day I'd be free. I'd get an apartment, settle down, get a mundane job...maybe someday starting a family."

I smiled, and as I did, I could feel my lips crack. "Zorin would've made a great father."

"Yeah," she choked out a laugh. "He would have been."

The door opened again. We clung to each other.

"Take this," I reached into my pocket and stuffed Teddy into her pocket. "If you live...I want you to have this."

"I'm not going to live."

"You're his daughter, Bells."

Yet another vampire rounded the corner, and he grinned at us. He looked at me, and his eyes glinted wickedly. "Your turn, little flower."

"No," I begged as he leaned down to unlock my chains from the wall. "Please."

"Don't take her," Bella shouted and shoved the vampire, but it didn't even sway him. He just smiled as he turned the key in the lock, and they crashed to the floor. "Don't take her!" she shouted, a little more loudly.

This time he punched her, and she yelped with pain.

"Bella!" I reached my hands over to touch her face, my loose chains rattling like metal snakes.

The vampire grabbed the back of my shirt and hauled me to my feet.

"Bella!" This time, her name was a plea for help.

"Don't!" She was crying again as she grasped my arms, as the vampire pulled me away in his. "Don't, please! Please! Rose!"

"Bella! Help me!" I was crying harder than ever as the vampire finally pulled me out of Bella's arms, into his. "Let me go!" I screeched. I turned as he carried me away, grabbing at his hair, punching his shoulder, but none of it helped.

"Oh, little flower," he purred as I sobbed. "We're doing this for your own good."

"Shut the fuck up," I cried.

We emerged from the dungeons.

If the dungeon was the first threshold of death, this hallway was the first room. The carpet and the walls were black. Every three feet on both my left and right sides were candelabras with red candles, dripping with red hot wax. At the end of the hall were tall dark doors that lead to the throne room. The vampire made no sounds as he approached the door.

It opened for us, and I let out a scream.

There were all my friends, dead on the floor. Lucy, Ginko, Zorin, Lucide, Alice, and Kat, all lying down on the carpet. Blood was seeping from their open wounds into the floor and all their faces were pale. Lucide and Ginko were limp next to the fireplace, Zorin was across the room discarded like trash next to the throne. Alice was at the Drainer's feet, and we passed Kat by the door, propped up against the wall, her leg bleeding.

The vampire laid me down next to Lucy, and I hugged her, sobbing. But then I froze. I could feel the faintest heartbeat under my fingers.

"You must be Rose."

I looked up into his face, and I wanted to swear, punch, kick, scream, but all I could do was look at him and ask, "Why are you doing this?"

"Because I can," he said, smiling with yellow teeth. "Watch."

He put his hand in a small puddle of blood near Lucy's head, and began soaking it up like a sponge. I watched in horror as the blood disappeared into his arm, his veins turning red, and his eyes a deep crimson.

When he straightened, he smiled at me with eyes of the devil.

His right hand thrust forward, and I'd felt I'd been punched in the gut as my body flew to the left, toward the hearth, where Lucide lay, crumpled and broken. My body slammed against his, but he gave no physical reaction. When I sat up I groaned, my head pounding. I reached over and felt a pulse in his neck, although I was careful my face stayed neutral.

"All your friends are dead."

I just looked at him. My mind raced. He didn't know I had felt pulses underneath my friend's skin. He must have known they weren't dead, but he was trying to leave me completely hopeless.

I'd never learned how to kill demons, but I doubted anything could live long after its throat was torn out.

I stood up. He smiled and cocked a finger. I was lifted about a foot off the ground and dragged toward him, through the air. He deposited me next to Lucy's still body.

"Do you know my favorite way of drawing blood from a human body, Rose? You can tear at the skin, break bones, but my favorite..."

He leaned down toward me, his teeth shining. "...is biting."

He took his hands and grasped my arms. I understood then what made Bella gasp in pain when he'd touched her. Even through the sleeve of my shirt, I could feel my skin burning, as if I had placed my arm on a hot stove. I struggled and shouted, but it was no use. He ducked his head down, and bit deeply into my upper right arm.

Pain shattered my reality, and I screamed. I could feel his teeth digging deeply into my muscle.

He drew back suddenly; his lips coated with my blood, dripping down his chin. His expression was confused, and he looked between Lucy and me, as I collapsed against her still body.

"You have the same blood," he said, mystified. "It tastes the same."

What in the hell was he talking about? I stroked Lucy's beautiful blonde hair, shaking her shoulder gently. She couldn't leave me, not now. I pressed against my arm where the Drainer had bitten me, the pain clouding my thoughts. Then she opened her eyes, and it hit me.

Green eyes. Blonde hair. The same blood. My father was the only other one I knew who looked like that. My heart started pounding, picking up on a whole new beat. Dad's journals that I had read a million years ago. When he said that Mom was pregnant, the baby wasn't me.

It was Lucy.

When reading the journals, I hadn't bothered to do the math. I had just assumed he meant the baby was me, but my parents were older than eighteen when they had me. They'd had a baby before me, and they must've lost her. I stroked her hair again, and when she looked at me, I saw our father in her green eyes.

Lucy tried to smile at me, and I helped her sit up. We would not face this alone.

The Drainer looked down on us, fascinated. "I found your

sister for you, Lucy."

Lucy looked at me, shocked and confused. I took her hand.

"Rose?" I heard a soft voice ask. I turned my head back to the fire—it was Ginko. He propped himself up on shaking elbows.

"Ginko!"

Ginko raised a shaking hand, and behind the Drainer, the throne began to tremble. The Drainer glanced back and laughed. "Cool party trick, kid." He flicked his fingers, and Ginko's head slammed against the wall. He slumped down again and was still.

"No!" I screamed.

The Drainer just laughed at me.

Zorin had woken up at my outburst, and he looked at me over the Drainer's shoulder. There was blood on his right temple, and his shirt was ripped at the shoulder. His hair was messy as if he'd had a bad night sleep. His eyes widened at me, and I read them almost too easily: Distract him.

I stood up, pulling Lucy with me. The Drainer raised his eyebrows.

When I took a step forward, he flicked his fingers, and again I was sent flying. Falling to the ground, I rolled, hitting the wall with a hard smack. I yelped as I felt what must've been one of my ribs crack.

"What were you planning on doing?" the Drainer called from across the room. "Hit me?"

That was all Zorin needed. He jumped on the Drainer's back, his arms tight around his neck. I saw his arms shaking from the pain of the skin-to-skin contact.

Caught by surprise, the Drainer's hands went to his throat as he staggered, trying to shake Zorin off his back. Zorin was screaming; the touch of the Drainer's skin must have hurt immensely. The Drainer fell on his right side, at the same time pulling one of Zorin's hands away from his throat, snapping his wrist like a twig. Zorin screamed as he fell, crushed partly by the Drainer's body weight.

When the Drainer straightened up, he leaned back down and bit Zorin's shoulder for good measure. Even from across the room, I could see the dark stain spreading across the black fabric of Zorin's shirt, a bite mark now embedded in his collar bone.

"There's one more thing I want to do before we begin," said the Drainer, and the bloodlust in his voice made my skin crawl. His yellow teeth gleamed, dripping with blood. He turned to the left and waved his hand in the air.

The air rippled—much like it did when I world jumped. I peered at the rippling and an image began to appear. The rippling got wider until it much resembled water rushing down a waterfall to a pool below. There were definite figures and faces in the illusion now. I blinked, and my eyes refocused.

"Rose!" The scream of my mother's voice shattered my world. She and Dad were standing together, identical horror on their faces as they saw where I was, finally, after nearly a month of separation.

"A gift for you, Rose," the Drainer whispered so quietly I could barely hear it. Of course, that was his tone of triumph: quiet and defiant, so you knew you were going to lose; you knew you had failed.

At the sound of his whisper, my parents turned their eyes to him.

"You bastard..." Mom started to say.

"Mom, Dad!" I screamed their names to get their attention back on me. This was the last time I was going to see them. I wanted to tell them I loved them.

"Rose..." Dad began, but then the image shattered into a million pieces like broken glass and my parents' images were gone.

I let out a strangled cry and sank to my knees. I felt someone embracing me and I turned. Lucy was hugging me, tears sliding down her nose.

"I thought you might want to see them one more time before I kill you." The Drainer smiled so widely he reminded me of a shark. And then that smile turned into a permanent hunting snarl. I knew it was going to be the last thing I saw.

I screamed as he lunged at me and—

Stopped.

He grunted.

A silver dagger was protruding out of the corroded blue flesh on his right shoulder, black blood—or whatever you would call it in a demon—oozing from the wound. I stared in amazement and horror as he pulled the dagger out slowly, the blade soiled by liquid evil.

"Hello, Father," said a familiar, dark voice.

I tried to twist my torso, but the movement was too painful. I used my arms to drag myself, and then I turned.

Bella, looking dark and dangerous, was standing tall and triumphant against the darkness, the firelight casting a shadow taller than she was. She had another dagger in her left hand. And Teddy, my little Teddy, was sitting on her shoulder, his tiny golden body arched like a cat in the presence of such a monster. There was magic in him after all.

"Bella... h-how did you...?"

"Teddy picked the lock for me," said Bella nonchalantly. "He's quite a useful little creature. I need to get myself one."

At her words Teddy crawled over her shoulder and curled around her ear, letting loose a tiny growl.

"That little thing picked the locks in my chain?" The Drainer asked incredulously. "Well. I guess I'll have to make them more durable."

"Where'd you get the knives?" I asked, staring at the shiny blade in Bella's hand.

Her eyes didn't stray from her father's. "I used to live here. I remember where my old room is."

"Well, my dear," the Drainer did a mock bow, "take your best shot."

Bella grinned and the bloody knife the Drainer had dropped flew off the floor and back into her hand. I looked sharply back at Ginko, who had sat up and was trying his best to help Bella, using his telekinesis as best he could in his weak state. The Drainer was too focused on his daughter to care about any assistance she might be getting.

As we watched, Teddy crawled down her arm and scuttled toward me, a tiny growl hissing between his teeth. I glanced back at the Drainer, but he was too busy staring at his daughter to notice a small dragon figurine crawling across the floor. I smiled when he walked onto my hand and made a motion with my head, telling him silently to start working with the chains.

With a grunt, Bella threw her knife at the Drainer, Ginko using telekinesis as leverage for speed. The Drainer dodged the speeding killer and came rushing at Bella.

She was prepared for this. Flipping the knife around so that it was a flash of silver, she thrust it into his stomach just as he was about to tackle her.

I would have cheered, but instead this new shift in the action made me gasp. I never thought the Drainer could be taken down this easily.

He groaned as Bella pulled the knife away. Just then, as if to close the matter, the second chain on my wrist clicked and fell off.

I felt an immense relief and sat there taking deep breaths. I could feel my strength returning, my power filling me.

The Drainer fell to his knees. He cried out in pain.

"This one's for Mom," Bella hissed and jabbed the dagger into her father's heart.

But then he smiled his yellow-toothed grin and the dagger Bella had stabbed into his chest fell to the floor.

Thrusting his arms into her chest, Bella flew backward and landed hard on the floor, next to Alice's unconscious body. He pulled the dagger out of the wound and the skin healed itself.

"You actually thought you could get rid of me that easily? Honestly, Erika, you should know me better than that."

Bella groaned and sat up.

"Had enough?" He was now holding the two daggers in his hand, waiting for her to do something.

"Honestly Father, you should know me better than that."

The Drainer smirked. "It's your move then."

Bella stood up. I held my breath. Right now we were all counting on her. I had no idea if the others would be able to fight and Teddy had only just moved on to Alice's chains. I was still gaining my strength back and I knew I didn't have enough gusto to handle a fight.

It was silent for a few moments as father and daughter stared each other down.

Bella's hands began to twitch. Her fingers jerked as if her hand had spasmed. It took me a moment to realize she was trying to use her water power.

Gaining enough power to form an icicle seemed to be too much for her. Sweat appeared on her brow, and she was breathing hard. At the last second, white blue light blinded us all, and the next second a large icicle was protruding from the Drainer's neck, having gone from Bella's hand right through his throat. He grunted, and with unsteady feet, she straightened up. He stood there with the ice in his throat.

I heard Bella gasp as the ice began to melt and I watched as the flesh of his throat healed itself. Water ran down his back.

"No..." I croaked as I saw him lean toward Bella. My chains shifted and with the little strength I possessed, I grabbed a chain and threw it. It landed with a hard thud on the Drainer's back.

He paused in his advance toward his daughter and turned around to grin at me—a look I'll never forget.

"I should've taken care of you first, you little bitch," he snarled.

Black gruesome tentacles came out of the sides of his body—three on each side—and shot at me, wrapping around me in a hold that had my lungs screaming for air and my muscles seeming to shred under the pressure.

"Rose!" Bella's voice sounded far off and seemed to crackle. My eardrums were about to shatter.

"Say goodbye to life, my darling," the Drainer cooed.

Then he screamed.

I was dropped to the floor and sweet, painful air leaked into my lungs. My hearing had turned back on, and the Drainer was still screaming. The tentacles he had tried to strangle me with were burning. The smell overwhelmed me, and I gagged.

I managed to turn my head toward the fireplace, knowing the only person who was able to use fire as a defense.

Lucide, looking half dead, had one hand in the fireplace and another aimed toward the Drainer. He had a look of concentration on his face. He didn't look at me; Teddy must have unlocked his chains as Bella and the Drainer were fighting.

All this gave Bella the few seconds she needed. She threw herself at the Drainer, shouting when their skin touched. She knocked him to the ground and they both went rolling. She ended up on top of him and punched him in the face. His head was whipped sideways. She punched again and a promising crack sounded.

Panting, she drew back her fists.

The smallest amount of black blood trickled out of his broken nose as he laughed. There was another sickening crunch as the bones healed.

"How many times do you have to try to hurt me to get the message? I can't die!"

He thrust his body up and Bella was blown backwards. She screamed, and as she hit the floor, she was instantly silenced.

"No!" I yelled.

The Drainer stood up and turned to me. "Don't worry, she's not dead. But you won't live long enough to see her again!"

Again, tentacles burst out of his sides and went for me. I knew now was the time to fight. I didn't have a chance, but I wasn't going to die lying at his feet sobbing. I stood up, holding my chain like a whip.

I swung my chain just as the tentacle was about to reach me, and they collided in mid air. Having the advantage, the Drainer pulled, and I yelped as I was yanked toward him.

If only I had a fire power like Lucide, I was thinking, I could make the chain really hot and he'd be forced to let go. I glanced at the floor frantically, looking for a way to plant my feet. There was nothing, but then something tiny and golden caught my eye. Teddy!

I knew what I had to do.

"Teddy!" I screamed. "NOW!"

I didn't need to explain, because Teddy's true function was not to pick locks.

It was to be a dragon.

I couldn't see him transform, but I could hear it. The floor shook, and what normally would be a tiny hiss became a tremendous roar of fury.

The Drainer dropped my chains and I fell backward.

Laying on my back I could see a golden underbelly, and strong muscular legs of what used to be my pet figurine.

The Drainer couldn't stop staring at the beast.

"Bella, get out of the way!" I called. She crawled to the side of the room. I could see all the others, awake now, also scrambling out of the way.

"Fire!"

I leapt out of the way just as Teddy released an incredibly awesome amount of flame at my enemy. His screams could be heard even over the crackling of the fire. I watched him burn, feeling like I was finally broken.

When the flames died, all that was left was a charred room and a pile of ash. Teddy shrunk back to figurine size, becoming still once more.

The humans in the room were silent, our enemy defeated.

When all the shock had worn down, I was burned out, with no energy, but we had work to do. I went over to my tiny dragon and picked him up. I hugged him briefly to my chest, and then tucked him away in my tattered pocket. My mind wanted to dwell on what he had done, how he had saved us, but we all had injuries that need to be treated. I turned slightly to the right to speak to Lucide. His hand was still in the fire.

"Lucide, get up," I said, pulling at his arm.

"I can't," he panted. "My leg..."

I looked down to see his leg had a gash, blood dripping onto the floor.

"Lucy! Come here and help me!" With my sister's help, we were able to lift Lucide up, an arm draped over each of our shoulders, his body mostly dead weight in the middle.

When we looked up, panting, about thirty vampires were blocking the exit. None of them looked ready to attack. They all looked at the Drainer's charred remains and the absolute ruin of the room. Then, one by one, they turned and exited the hall in silence.

"Well that was eventful," I heard Ginko mutter.

I didn't have time right now to worry about fickle vampires. I turned to Lucide. "Come on, Lucide, you can do it!" I said as we began to walk forward.

"Did I ever tell you I love you?" he joked dryly as we dragged him. Despite our situation and the fact that it was a joke, my heart thumped and I felt my cheeks burn as Lucy looked at me.

"Can you make it, Bella?" I asked to distract myself.

"Yeah," she said, getting off the ground. "I'll be fine. The worst I'll have is bruises." There was nothing more she could do to help Lucide, but she hovered over him nonetheless.

"You're going to have to play nurse soon," I said, trying to smile.

Just then Crissy came around the corner and rushed to Bella. "Erika! I heard a loud noise and then all the vampires just..." It was then that she looked behind us and saw what remained of the throne room. "Is...is that?"

"Yes," said Bella bluntly. "Listen to me, Crissy. Gather all the servants you can find, and get out of here. We don't know if the vampires will make a reappearance."

She nodded, but before she rushed off, she turned to back to Bella and said, completely genuinely, "I'm sorry about your father, Erika."

Bella just nodded. "Take care of yourself." They hugged briefly, and Crissy ran off.

Looking back, I have no idea how we got out of the palace without us collapsing from exhaustion. We just kept moving, and poor, tired Alice flew ahead of us to find a place to stay. We wouldn't have been able to do it without her.

By the time we got to an inn, Lucide was barely conscious. We convinced the innkeeper to give us a room with clean beds and fresh water in exchange for a performance once we healed. Seeing how desperate we were, he obliged, and gave us the biggest room the inn had.

Everyone drank water right away. The water Crissy had brought us had been the only liquid we'd had since experiencing the nightmare. Bella drank the most, guzzling five glasses. After about a half an hour, she went about treating all our injuries. It exhausted her. We were all exhausted. Lucide lay in the middle of the bed, sweating and panting as Bella laid her hands on his leg, her hands already stained with blood.

"Stay with me, Lucide, stay with me," she chanted as the skin began to heal. He moaned and squeezed my hand, which he had been clutching for a while now.

"Almost done!" Bella cried as he gave another strangled scream and almost broke my hand. "We're almost done!"

"You remind me of a pregnant woman giving birth," I said, trying to distract him from the pain.

He spoke between labored breaths. "Boy or girl, darling?"

"Oh, I definitely want another Lucide," I said, smiling and rolling my eyes.

"Ha ha, OW...!" he yelped. We all heard a sickening crunch as his bones fit back together. He sat there, panting. The grip on my arm loosened.

"It's over," said Bella, smiling faintly. She looked the most exhausted of us all.

"Go to sleep, Bella," I said. "You did it."

Without a single protest—which was so unlike her—Bella fell into the other bed and didn't move.

"I'm going to see if we can get some food," Alice whispered. She and Ginko ghosted out of the room together. Lucy was beyond reviving at the table, Kat was curled up on the floor, and Zorin went to lie next to Bella. I was left with Lucide. If I hadn't been so tired, I would've noticed he had no shirt on.

"Congratulations," he whispered. "It's a boy."

"What are we naming him?" I asked, taking his hand and laying my head against his chest. His hands were like ice.

"Derek," he said.

"That's too common," I said, wrinkling my nose.

"What would you name our boy whom I so dutifully labored over?"

"Lucide," I said, snuggling closer into his chest. I could hear his heart beating.

He snorted. "Like the world needs more of me."

"It does," I said, slipping out of our game. "You saved my life."

"It's my job," he said, just as serious.

"You didn't need to. It would be different if it were someone from the gang, but it was me. The outcast. The freak.

The sideshow. You chose to save my life."

"Is that how you see yourself?" he said, shifting his weight and trying to look down at me.

"Yes. I popped out of nowhere, and you're expected to take me in. A rugged family who can hardly support themselves, let alone a tag-a-long."

"We support ourselves just fine."

"I didn't mean that," I said, reversing. "I just meant that you had no obligation to take me in. I'm a stranger."

"Not anymore." And to my great delight and surprise, he kissed my forehead.

"But I was at the time," I persisted.

"Rose." He got out from under me, letting my head drop on the pillow, and he was suddenly on top of me, hovering over me. The muscles in his arms contracted, almost seemed to ripple, and I could tell even this action was too much for him. I felt lost in the depths of his eyes as he stared me down.

"I might not make it to the morning, so let's just enjoy the time we have together."

"What do you mean?" I snapped. "Of course you're going to make it!"

"No Rose. I'm weak, cold, and my heart beat is slow. I might not make it."

"Yes you will," I said. "You have to."

"I'm going to try and hang on," he said. "I want to be there for you when you go back home."

"I'm not going home. Not after this."

"Listen to me, Rose! You are going home. You have to. I would never forgive myself if I was holding you here. Promise me that even if I die in the morning you'll go back home."

"You won't die!"

"Promise me!"

"Bull-shit!"

"Rose!" he had tears in his eyes now, something I'd never seen happen. "Promise me..."

"I will. Fine. I'll go home."

"Good." He lay down on his side, facing me, using his elbow to keep his head up. "Bella should have picked a stronger leader."

"You're the strongest person I know."

"You're stronger."

And that's when he kissed me.

My first kiss. And it was the most powerful, wonderful thing I'd ever felt. All the warmth from Lucide's fire seemed to flow through his lips as they moved with mine, hungry, and yearning to be wanted and loved.

When he let go of me, I had almost forgotten my name.

"Sleep now," he said. "I'll still be here in the morning."

"You better be, otherwise I'll haunt your ass," I mumbled sleepily.

I fell asleep to quiet laughter rumbling from his chest.

The next morning was like waking up from a week in hell. I shifted and groaned. I needed food. Raising my head, I saw Alice had kept good to her promise. On the table was an assortment of cereals, fruit and bread. I smiled and lay my head back down.

That was when my brain fully registered.

Lucide! My head shot up and I looked at his face. He was still and his skin seemed cooler than usual. I began to shake him.

"Lucide? Lucide!"

He didn't move. I felt for a pulse and felt nothing.

"No! Bella! Bella, wake up!"

In the second it took her to reply, I was afraid I was in a room with seven dead bodies.

"What is it?" asked Bella alarmed, and I could breathe again.

"I can't feel a pulse," I sobbed.

"Move back," Bella commanded.

I did as I was told and stumbled into Lucy's arms, sobbing. She held me and stroked my hair.

"I'm going to bring the Drainer back from hell to murder him a second time," I whimpered.

She continued to stroke my hair.

Bella had her hand on Lucide's chest, closing her eyes and focusing. "Don't give up on me now, Lucide," I heard her whisper.

"Because I'll haunt your ass," I murmured into Lucy's chest. "I promised you that."

"No one wants Rose haunting them," said Bella. "Come on, Lucide, come on..."

My heart stopped as I heard a strangled gasp. Lucide's eyes were open and blinking furiously.

"Oh, Bella, you did it," I cried, throwing my arms around her neck.

"I wish you hadn't done that," said Lucide, his breathing back to normal. "I was sleeping."

"Oh, you idiot," I said throwing my arms around his neck. "You were dead! How could you? You promised me."

"I didn't promise you anything, beautiful. I just didn't want you haunting my ass."

"Rose always goes through with her promises," said Bella smiling.

"And I would have with this one. I mean, how could you do that to me? Kiss me and then die? I mean, honestly that was the most cruel, selfish thing I've ever seen you do... "

He interrupted me with a kiss, wrapping his arms around me and falling on the bed.

Wolf whistles and hollers filled the room as my head spun.

"Breakfast everyone!" Alice sang when we finally broke. "Unless the two love birds want to go back to bed."

I blushed and everyone laughed. I helped Lucide out of the bed, and we went to have breakfast at the crowded hotel table.

After breakfast I felt stronger than I had in days. I laced my fingers with Lucide's, happy to be alive and together.

Empty plates were on the floor, and cups were empty of water and juice. There wasn't an extra scrap of food. It made me sad. We'd always be hungry. Then my back stiffened when I remembered my promise and Lucide squeezed my hand.

I couldn't.

I looked at Lucide with pleading eyes, but he shook his head and nodded toward Lucy. Her eyes were distant and sad. I couldn't forget about her. She was my sister, and had been robbed of her family for twenty years.

I took a deep breath and then realized that the whole room had gone silent. They knew it was time, too.

Tears streamed down Lucy's cheeks. I gritted my teeth.

"I can't!" I cried. I resisted the urge to burst into tears.

Lucide put his arm around me. "You have to."

"Shut up!" All the romance of the moment was shattered, and he looked hurt. "No one can tell me what to do!"

"I can," said Bella softly. "You have to go home, Rose."

"No."

Lucy put her hand on my arm and slid a note toward me. *Don't you miss them?*

My resistance broke; I burst into tears. I thought of Mom, Dad, and Jasmine. I remembered their faces when they saw me lying on the ground, bleeding and broken. I thought of how they would look when they found me alive and finally get Lucy back... yes. Yes, I missed them. Why did I have to say it?

I stayed silent, crying.

"We'll be fine," said Bella. "We can rent an apartment, keep performing. You should go home."

"You're trying to get rid of me that fast?" I asked coldly. "I thought you liked me."

Bella's eyes flashed. "Of course I like you, Rose, but right now you're making it difficult."

"It just feels like you're trying to brush us off when we're part of your family. And Lucy's been with you for years..."

"I'm not trying to brush you..."

"Shut up..."

"Now you listen here, Rose King..."

Someone banged on the table, sending all the empty plates and cups bouncing.

We turned toward Lucy, who—for the lack of better words—looked pissed off. She looked back and forth between Bella and me expectantly.

I took a deep breath. "I'm sorry, Bella."

"Me too."

We were silent for a few minutes.

"Let's make a plan first," said Bella. "Then you two need to go home."

I felt sick, but nodded.

"First we need to perform for the inn. Then..." she paused, staring at us.

"What is it?" Zorin asked gently.

"There's something I'd like to do," she said looking at her hands. "I've never done this before, because, well, the Drainer would've...something could've happened." She took a deep breath. "You all know my secret now, that the Drainer was my father. He was a demon. Which makes me half demon. My mother was human. I know a spell that could...it-it could..." She couldn't finish, and I understood why.

"Then you need to become human," I said gently.

She smiled at me and touched the scar on her arm. "I need to become human."

We cleaned up; then went to pay our debt.

We retreated to the woods after we performed for a second time that day, bringing in large sum of money. Lucy and I both knew it'd be the last time we performed with the Rags and Riches gang, so we tried to play our best. I sang along with her violin, but my heart just wasn't in it. Knowing this was the last time I would be performing made my heart sink instead of sing. Bella seemed to recognize this, and offered to buy me something special.

"You keep the money," I said, trying to smile. "Start saving up for that glorious apartment." I paused for a moment and then reached into my pocket, taking out Teddy. I put him in Bella's hand. "You keep him," I said. "If I really am leaving, he'll be something to remember me by."

She smiled and put the money and Teddy away in the backpack.

Instead of a fire like we normally built when we settled down for the night, Bella took a stick and took her time drawing a pentagram in the dirt. I watched her for signs of nervousness, but she seemed perfectly calm.

"Each tip represents something," she said in a hushed whisper once she'd brushed away the excess dirt. "Water, fire, earth, air, and spirit. I'm going to need your help on this one,

Lucide."

Lucide nodded, watching her as carefully as I was. We arranged ourselves in a circle, around the pentagram.

Bella knelt and began the ritual.

"I call on my father's spirit to ask for permission to perform this ritual."

A chilling breeze rose up, and circulated around her. Goosebumps raised the hairs on my neck.

"I call on the earth to support me."

The ground trembled to acknowledge its acceptance.

"I call on the air to help me fly."

Again, wind swirled around us, but it was a warm summer breeze.

"I call on fire for warmth and strength." She reached for Lucide's hands and gripped them hard. The pentagram exploded with orange fire, lighting their faces, creating a blast of heat. They let go of each other; the pentagram continued to burn.

"Lastly I call on water for power and love."

For a few seconds, nothing happened. Then the pentagram filled with water, flooding the fire. Bella frowned. There was this shifting sound as the water turned to ice.

I gasped; Lucide squeezed my hand in warning.

Moments passed with nothing. Bella tilted her head heavenward.

Power exploded.

That's what it felt like. A powerful surge of energy rose up and pushed out, almost knocking us off our feet. The ice in the pentagram cracked, the sound like a death cannon.

I watched, mesmerized.

Shards of ice as sharp as needles came out of the pentagram.

Bella stood up, her eyes still closed, and waited.

The ice shards flew toward her like darts.

I tried to scream, but the sound wouldn't come out of my throat. They were going to kill her!

The shards bit into her flesh and sank into her skin. No blood was drawn. She grunted, her face looking disturbed.

Then, very slowly, she began to rise off the ground.

At her torso, her core, light began to glow. It was a white light, like a light at the end of a tunnel. It continued to gain strength and engulf her entire body. It reminded me of Alice's wing transformation.

Once her entire body was swallowed by the light, it got stronger. It burned my eyes. I covered my face with my hands. When I opened them again, she was on the ground, lying on her side, all the light gone. At her feet, the pentagram had turned into a yin yang.

Zorin went over to her. "Bella?"

She sat up and lifted up her sleeve.

There was no more scar.

"It worked. . ." she smiled, and then tipped over, her head landing on Zorin's shoulder.

"We need to talk," I said in Lucide's ear. "I'll go buy some food," I said a little louder. "Bella's going to want something when she wakes up."

Zorin nodded, and I took the backpack, grasped Lucide's hand, and started walking back towards town.

We were silent for a little while; all I could hear was the sound of our footsteps on the gravel. It reminded me of a day in September, walking with Jasmine along a lonely road.

"Why did you do it?" I asked.

"What do you mean?" asked Lucide.

"Why did you kiss me?"

"I like you, Rose."

"You knew all along I was planning to leave when I could," I said, getting angry. "I was temporary. Do you know how hard it's going to be to leave now that I...I have feelings for you?"

He tried to smile as he kept pace with me. When he didn't answer, I stopped.

"My God, Lucide." Was he just stalling, or did he really not understand my point?

"You're such a mystery sometimes, Rose."

"How is that a mystery? I came. I was planning to leave. The worst is over. Now I'm leaving. Is that really so hard to follow?"

"No, I..."

"Then why'd you kiss me, when you knew I couldn't stay?"

"I was hoping you wouldn't have to."

His reply sent me reeling. "What?"

"I was hoping Lucy wasn't your sister. I was hoping you wouldn't miss home. I was hoping you'd stay."

"That is the most selfish thing I've ever heard you say."

He shrugged. "I left home and didn't miss it so much."

"Yes you do. You're just too quiet to show it."

He looked down. Then for the second time since I knew him, he had tears in his eyes.

"I don't have anyone. I was hoping you would be the one to stay."

I kissed him, surprised by my own boldness. "Come with us."

That made him smile a little. "I can't leave. I have a family here."

One look in his eyes told me he had made a decision just as hard as mine. He would stay for his family, and I would leave for my sister. "Then you have someone," I said quietly.

"Are you going to get the food, or are you going to leave Bella starving?"

I smiled and picked up the pace.

When we got back to the camp, everything was set to the familiar rhythm. Bella was awake and leaning against Zorin's chest. Ginko was poking a stick at the new fire, and Alice had her wings spread out. Kat was twitching her tail impatiently. The yin yang symbol was still there.

They all looked up when we got back. I dropped the bag on the floor.

"I used as little money as I could. The food should last you a few days."

"Thank you," said Bella, getting up. "We'll get an apartment, figure something out."

I nodded; I couldn't look her in the eye.

Suddenly she came over and hugged me. "You saved us. We couldn't have done this without you." She turned and hugged Lucy next, whispered something in her ear, and stepped back.

The goodbyes were horrible. Some resentful, bitter part of

myself was telling me I didn't have to do this. I could stay here forever and be a part of something that used to be untouchable to me, but I had to be strong. My family was waiting for me in another world, and I'd kept Lucy waiting long enough.

I went numb until I said goodbye to Lucide. He'd hugged Lucy first, and then turned to me. I'll never forget the look in his eyes—they were blazing—as he leaned down and kissed me.

It was the softest, most loving kiss.

I turned and took Lucy's hand, trying my hardest not to cry.

I thought of home. I thought of the Little Library, my parents, and Jasmine. I thought of my room, and of the warm breeze that would brush my cheeks as I walked to school.

The air warmed. I felt the earth slowly shifting as we drifted away.

"Goodbye," I whispered as everything faded.

Where we had stood bloomed a single red rose.

Chapter 12: Family

We landed in my front yard.

I landed on my side at the last second. I'd seen the ground fast approaching and twisted. Lucy landed next to me, on her side as well.

The front door opened.

I heard a sound burst from my mother that was half way between a sob and a scream. I welcomed any sound from her; it meant I was home. She ran toward us, tears already dripping down her cheeks, tripping over her feet as she rushed to embrace us. Dad was right behind her, his eyes on the pair of us with our ripped clothing and starved eyes. He was sobbing too.

The next thing I knew I was being crushed in his arms. Then Mom collided into us, and we were all sobbing and holding each other.

Finally, when we pulled away, I stopped their rush of question by introducing Lucy.

"I want you to meet someone."

Lucy stood there, staring at our parents.

"This is Lucy," I said. "My sister."

Dad paled. Mom looked like she was going to faint.

"She has your eyes, Andrew," Mom whispered, as she gazed at Lucy.

Dad looked at her. Her build, the color of her hair, and her green eyes. Then, he said finally, "Is that you, darling?" A tear leaked out of his eye.

Lucy nodded.

As he went to embrace her, he was shaking.

"My God, you've grown. Has it really been twenty years? Damn, I'm old."

"Andrew," said Mom. She went over to Lucy. "How did you...?"

"Lucy can't speak," I said, my own throat tight.

Mom began to cry and hugged Lucy hard. "How did you find out you had a sister? We never told you."

"It's a long story," I said. Not one I wanted to revisit so soon. "Please, Mommy," I begged.

She seemed to understand. "Let's go inside," Dad said, putting his arms around me as I began to sob.

We went inside, together as a whole for the first time in twenty years.

In no time at all, Lucy was welcomed back home. As emotional as it was, Dad explained to Lucy that they never gave her up or abandon her, she had been kidnapped. In desperation, he showed her his journals, the entry that announced Charlotte's pregnancy when she was eighteen, but their gracious homecoming was all Lucy needed. She was home.

Of course, questions still lingered for all of us. Who had taken her, and why? There were significant gaps in Lucy's memory. She didn't remember a thing about being taken, or life as a young child. We were all curious, but we didn't press the idea. None of us wanted to trigger an unwanted, unpleasant memory.

Once she'd been home for about a week, Mom and Dad organized a small get together so Lucy could meet all the friends and family.

I helped Mom bake a cake. Dad was busy cleaning the living room and Lucy was in her room getting ready.

"I'm going to check on Lucy," I said, washing my hands.

"Tell her they'll start arriving in ten minutes," Mom said.

"OK!" I called as I ran up the stairs.

I knocked on Lucy's door. "Lucy? Can I come in?"

I opened the door to find my sister sitting on her bed, looking down at the carpet.

"Hey." I sat down on the bed next to her, and the mattress sunk under my added weight. I put my hand over hers. "What's wrong?"

She took a piece of paper out of her pocket and started writing. *I've never done this before.*

"I know," I said, trying to catch her eye. "But this is your family. It'll be fine."

That's just it. They don't feel like my family.

I wish I could've said I know what you mean, but I

couldn't. I had always lived with my family, and no one else, until very recently. This must be very hard for my sister.

"But they will," I promised. "And there will be cake!"

She perked up at that idea. I got sad when I realized just how little she might've eaten cake—or any kind of treat—in her old life.

Just then the doorbell rang. I pulled my sister to her feet and led her downstairs.

Everyone was overjoyed to see Lucy again; there wasn't a dry eye for quite a while. But then Lucy began writing funny stories about the Rags and Riches gang to make everyone laugh. She seemed to be getting over her nervousness. She would even look over, smiling at me once or twice. I tried to smile back, but I was impatient. I had invited Jasmine over to meet Lucy, and she hadn't arrived yet. We had gotten hold of Wendy and Jack, and I knew Jasmine would want to meet some fellow vampires. I was just hoping Lucy would take the fact that vampires were coming to the party well.

Lucy wasn't used to Wendy yet. She kept her distance. They seemed to understand, and didn't push themselves on her. I had explained to them the only vampires Lucy had known had tried to kill her multiple times.

The cake was passed out. I began to tap my foot.

The doorbell rang. I ran to it and wrenched the door open. Jasmine was standing there, looking breathtaking in a simple blue dress that flowed around her knees, silver sequins at the collar.

"Rose!" her face lit up when she saw me. She flung her arms around me. "You're back! You're really back! I missed you so much!"

I hugged her back, and suddenly her tardiness wasn't important anymore. "I missed you too. Come on, you're just in time for cake." I pulled her into the kitchen.

"Jasmine! Good to see you, honey," said Dad, coming into the hallway. "We were worried you weren't going to make it."

"Good to see you too, Mr. King."

"Lucy!" Dad called over his shoulder. "There's someone else I want you to meet."

That's when I remembered I hadn't warned my sister that

yet another vampire was joining us. "Dad, I don't think that's such a good..."

"This is Jasmine, Rose's friend."

Lucy's eyes widened when she saw Jasmine. Her pale skin, her eyes, and the slightly sharper teeth as she tried to smile. I could tell she was shaking slightly as she shook Jasmine's hand.

"Nice to meet you, Lucy," said Jasmine kindly, smiling at her.

Lucy smiled timidly, trying not to shrink back.

"Let's go upstairs," I said cheerfully to Jasmine. I grabbed her hand and we ran up the stairs into the Little Library.

"She hates me," said Jasmine, once the door was closed.

"That wasn't you," I said. "You have to understand, she's only known vampires as killers. She just has to get used to you."

"I know. I won't push it."

"Thank you."

"Can we go back downstairs? Or are you going to keep me prisoner in the library forever?"

"Death by books," I grinned. "How tragic."

"Absolute torture."

We grinned at each other.

It was good to see her smiling, actually smiling, and have no worry about anything. No school or secrets. I was actually truly, back home. I would sleep in a bed tonight and not on a cold forest floor. My smile faltered when I thought about Bella and the others. I couldn't help but think we'd abandoned them. Lucy had been part of that family forever. We had left them as street performers while we had a roof over our heads and cake in the kitchen. I tried to send the thoughts away; now that the Drainer was gone they finally had a chance to get back on their feet.

Wendy and Jack were the last ones to leave. Wendy seemed on edge. Her eyes wouldn't settle on things, and she fidgeted. Dad noticed, and told me to go up to my room.

"But Dad, what..."

"Now, Rose."

I shrank back. Lucy had already gone upstairs to take a shower. Jasmine was waiting for me in the Little Library. Dashing up the stairs, I tried to be as quiet as I could. I slipped inside the library, the door making a loud click. I winced.

"Hi," said Jasmine, looking up for the book she was reading. "What took you so long?"

"Shh!" I hushed. "Wendy and Jack are downstairs, talking to my parents. I want to find out what they're talking about."

"That's the Rose I know," said Jasmine, shutting the book and coming over to me. "What do we do?"

I motioned toward an air duct just behind the door. The sound of voices drifted up, but I couldn't hear anything specific.

"I can't hear what's going on down there," I whispered.

"I can," Jasmine whispered. She was posed, one ear leaning toward the sound of muffled voices, the book forgotten beside her.

"Of course you can," I muttered. Why did she get to have all the fun?

"Please, shut up," Jasmine pleaded. "I can't focus." She started repeating what the adults downstairs were saying to me just seconds after they said it themselves.

"Wendy, Jack, please sit down." Jasmine's voice had the deepness of my father's.

"What's going on, Andrew? You're scaring me," said Jasmine, switching to Wendy.

"There's nothing to be worried about," said my mom's voice.

"Charlotte's right, we just have some news to tell you," said Dad.

"What is it?" Jasmine turned to an even deeper voice— Jack's

"When we were kids," Dad began, "well, when Charlotte and I were kids, rather—you told us the story about your human life."

When my parents and Wendy had met, my parents had only been teenagers and Wendy a vampire—changed at the age of eighteen. While the years went by and changed my parents in looks and age, Wendy had stayed forbiddingly beautiful at eighteen years old.

"Yes?" Wendy's voice asked.

"You told us how you got married, settled down, and had

a child...Jasmine, right?"

Jasmine stiffened. I copied her, afraid of her reaction.

Wendy's voice was full of anger. "Why are you bringing this up, Andrew? You know I don't like talking about her."

Jasmine pulled back. "I don't want to hear any more."

"She just doesn't like talking about you because she thinks you were killed. It's a painful subject for her. Please Jasmine." I tried to make my voice kind but a tone of pleading had leaked into it.

"You knew about this? You knew I was their child and didn't say anything!"

"No, it's not like that..."

"What the hell is it like, then?"

"Dad started to piece it together. Please Jasmine."

Taking a deep breath, Jasmine began to listen again.

"We told you Rose went to a new school this year. She made a lot of new friends and brought a girl home one night. That girl's name was Jasmine."

There was silence in the room. Jasmine and I waited, barely breathing.

"She came over a lot; she and Rose became really good friends. When Rose got that letter from you, Jasmine had already started to put two and two together. I started to read her mind and realized she was your daughter."

Jasmine didn't wait to tell me what was happening next. She was out of her room with vampire speed. I ran after her down the stairs and into the kitchen.

When I arrived, heart thumping and mind racing, Jasmine was in front of me, staring at her parents and they were staring back.

"Mother...Father?"

They kept staring at each other. Wendy's eyes were wide with disbelief, and Jack looked stunned.

"Jasmine? Is that you, baby?" Wendy's voice was cautiously gentle.

Tears were streaming down Jasmine's face. I had never seen her so heartbroken. There were tears in Wendy and Jack's eyes too, while my parents and I stood frozen in our places.

Wendy walked slowly up to Jasmine with Jack not far behind. She touched Jasmine's pale white face and looked into her fierce, sly eyes.

"That's my hair," she said, touching the black river that was flowing down Jasmine's back. She touched her white cheek again. "They turned you into a vampire."

"Does that mean you don't want me?" her voice was thick with panic.

"Of course not, darling." Wendy's voice had taken on a motherly coo I'd never heard her use before. "Of course we want you."

Slowly, staring at her mother all the while, Jasmine leaned her head against Wendy's chest and sighed. Even more slowly, Wendy folded her arms around her only daughter and started sobbing. Jack reached over and started lovingly petting Jasmine's raven hair.

That's when I moved over to my parents to watch with them. Dad put his arms around me, while my Mom's arm was around his waist. We watched the family reunion from our small corner of the kitchen.

After all the tears were over, the small family thanked us and left. Jasmine smiled at me happily, and I tried to smile back just as warmly, but couldn't. Her happiness couldn't change that I felt like I was losing my best friend. She had a family now who would take up all her time. What would she need me for?

A few weeks went by and still I heard nothing from Jasmine, Wendy or Jack. I tried to keep my mind off it, but I still missed her terribly.

I was helping Dad clean the library—I had made a mess of it in my boredom. Books were everywhere around the room, stacked in piles, open to random pages, dog-eared, turned upside down. Within a few hours I felt like I'd read the whole library and was fed up with it all. Dad insisted I clean it up and offered to help when I had complained. We could have cleaned it up in seconds by magic, but I think he wanted to give me time to tell him what was bothering me out loud.

The afternoon sun was shining through the window as I

picked up three thick books I'd left lying on the window seat. I remembered feeling like throwing them across the room when the stories hadn't turned out the way I wanted them to. My grip tightened on the spine and I quickly put them on the shelf to stop myself from going into a complete rage.

"You've been quiet," Dad said. I turned to look at him. He had a book in his hand, but he was looking at me, watching the emotions play across my face.

"It's nothing," I said, avoiding his eye and picking up another book I had left open.

"It doesn't look like nothing. What's bothering you?"

"I just miss Jasmine," I confessed, sliding the book into place. "It's been three weeks. How long is she going to shut me out?"

"They've been apart for more than three weeks. And Jasmine isn't shutting you out—she just needs to be with her family."

"Well it's not like I haven't been through something too! I just got back from being in another world where this blood-crazed demon tried to kill me and my sister! I need her right now."

"She knows that." I still had my back to him, my hands gripping the shelves as angry tears filled my eyes.

"It doesn't seem like she does."

"Rose, Jasmine had been with you since you first met. She wouldn't just drop out now. You've your family to support you through your ordeal while she hasn't had her family to support her through her life for three hundred years."

"That long?" Jasmine had never told me she was that old.

"It's been a long and painful journey for all of them," he said softly.

I had never even considered that Jasmine was so old. With each passing day we had spent together had changed me in ways that it hadn't her. She would be sixteen years old for another fifty years, another hundred. And by then, I would be dead.

"Dad?"

"Hm?"

I looked over at him. He had sat himself cross-legged on

the floor, a book open in his lap.

"Dad," I scolded, taking the book from him and crawling into his lap like a small child. "What were you reading?" I closed the book to look at the front cover but it had no title. That's when I recognized the design, the binding and inside, the handwriting.

I gulped.

Dad wrapped his arms around me. "You read my journals, didn't you?"

"Yes." How could I lie to him when he could read the truth in my thoughts? My mind burned with the guilt I carried by reading private property.

"That's alright. I was wondering when you would. It didn't happen to change your mind over keeping a journal yourself, would it?"

I made a face and knew he could read the disgust in my thoughts. Then my mind went to a different topic entirely, and I could feel his arms stiffen around me.

"Dad?" I looked down and started twirling a bit of brown hair between my fingers.

"Yes?" he asked cautiously.

"Did Wendy ever offer to turn you into a vampire?"

"She did—more than once, in fact."

I was very surprised by his answer, although that was just like her. "How old were you?"

"I was sixteen when she first offered."

I shifted suddenly. Would Jasmine really...?

His arms tightened suddenly, holding me so close I could barely breathe.

"I was only thinking Dad. Stay out of my head, would you?" What was the point of even having the conversation aloud if he was getting cheat sheets?

"I'm not trying to read your thoughts, they just come to me."

I had to accept that. My dad wouldn't try to invade my privacy. Instead I thought of Jasmine and Lucy, and the Rags and Riches gang. They had really meant a lot to me. They had kept me sane in a time when I was completely entitled to go insane.

"You miss them."

I twisted in his arms to look at his face. His eyes were glassy, almost shining, as he watched the scenes going on in my head like a movie.

I wanted to feel angry with him—upset—but I couldn't. The scenes kept playing in my mind, like a colorful dance; the partners inviting me to come and dance with them. And oh, how well I danced! I saw Lucy playing on her violin, the music her voice. Me singing in a sparkling gown that was only an eye pleaser, a small city crowd cheering, the sound of coins falling with soft clanks. I saw meat roasting over the fire of the gang-camp, the delicious smell making my stomach growl with the hunger that was ever-present. I saw the scar of the Drainer's name etched into Bella's arm and the sour face she had when I realized her secret. I saw her being changed from half-demon into a full-human; the air humming with magic, singing with it, her transformation complete. When she pulled back the sleeve of her arm to show pale unblemished white skin . . .

The last thing I thought of made me blush: when Lucide, his blue eyes blazing, had leaned down and given me a gentle good-bye kiss.

Dad hugged me softly this time, holding me in his arms as my thoughts shattered and the tears finally overflowed, running down my face.

Dad spoke in my ear. "You know now that my stories aren't just made up. You read all about the battles I fought, the friends that I made, and the sacrifices I had to make. I made a choice once when I was your age. I had a life waiting for me in this world. I needed to make a choice if I wanted it or not. If I accepted, I would have a life unlike anything else. It was the hardest decision I ever had to make."

I swallowed, trying to stop my voice from breaking. "Do you regret it?"

He turned me around in his arms, kissing my forehead and then piercing me with his fierce eyes. "No." It was the most sure thing I had ever heard him say.

"So what are you telling me exactly?" I wiped the tears from my face. "I should go back?"

"I'm telling you that when you're old enough, your options are open."

I snuggled against his chest, his chin resting on my hair. "I love you," I said.

"I love you, too."

Somehow, that love was enough to keep me anchored.